SKINNERS

a novel

by Will Forest

Respondióle el marinero,
tal respuesta le fue a dar:
—Yo no digo esta canción
sino a quien conmigo va.
"Romance del Conde Arnaldos"

Que es mi barco mi tesoro,
que es mi dios la libertad,
mi ley, la fuerza y el viento,
mi única patria, la mar.
José de Espronceda

The happy ending still beckons,
and it is in hope of grasping it
that we go on.
Annie Proulx

I think hard times are coming
when we will be wanting
the voices of writers who can see
alternatives to how we live now,
and even imagine some real grounds for hope.
Ursula K. Le Guin

Table of Contents

Prologue

August 22, 1662

Cartagena de Indias, Kingdom of Nueva Granada

A pearly mist rolled in low from the south, covering the Bay of Las Animas with all the comfort of a wet sheet. It arrived so quick and so thick that when Eddie Fife turned around with another load, he could no longer see the crates he had just stacked on the pier a mere ten feet in front of him. Not half an hour earlier, sweating under the last minutes of the day's dose of Caribbean sunshine, he had removed his linen shirt and laid it over a railing, but now the suddenly cold and moist air around his torso made him shiver. He felt the heat recede from the silver locket against his chest.

"This fog will last long into the night," yelled the first mate. "All hands back on board! Except you, Fife! Help me lash down these crates. We'll move them tomorrow morning once we can see what we're doing."

Eddie could barely make out the shape of the first mate approaching until he was right next to him. The two men hoisted the heaviest chain they could find, with a sturdy lock, to protect the cargo through the night. As they passed the links left and right around the pile, the sun dropped fast and the fog grew heavier. Soon there was only a weak moon to cast its milky pall through the sieve of the fog. A few lights shone from the quarters of the sailors already back aboard the *Summit of Virtue*, and the cobblestone streets of Cartagena began to light up as a watchman moved from lantern to lantern.

Floating eerily through the mist came a sound that ebbed and flowed like the tide… bits of a song that Eddie could hear in moments when the chain wasn't clanking. It was a lilting tune that carried easily through the dense, wet air, tickling his ears and setting his teeth on edge.

"Mr. Higgins… Is that… someone singing?"

The first mate froze, alert. "Aye," he whispered. "A woman's voice. Listen... Can you reckon where she is?"

Eddie turned his head, looking blindly around the pier. "It seems like it's coming from all around us."

The first mate clenched his jaw and gave a quick nod. "That be the Sea Witch, I wager. I've heard tell she appears only in the fog, because naught else can cloak her."

"What is she singing?"

"A spell, you fool," whispered Mr. Higgins as he squatted behind the crates. "Duck down here and keep quiet."

Eddie crouched down, his senses keen. In the eighteen months since he'd left Bristol, he'd never heard of a sea witch. But then again, the life of adventure he'd imagined when he signed on with a shipping company had become nothing but long hours of hardship and tedium. Even the past few days in Cartagena had yielded little joy. Detained by the Spanish authorities, he and the rest of the crew had finally been released on bail with a heavy fine and the contingency of a week's quarantine on board their ship. But a witch, well… at least this, he could rightly call an adventure.

The woman's high melody spun through the suspended droplets of mist around them, suddenly much closer. She was humming now.

Then there was another sound… a percussion accompaniment of sorts. Someone was walking toward them down the pier—heavy, strong footsteps that surely did not belong to the same person as the high, sweet voice, Eddie thought. It seemed that a man had come to meet the witch.

The footsteps and the humming stopped together, and a dialogue began. Eddie could hear every word they said yet could understand nothing. What language was this? He could only guess by tone of voice that their transaction was rushed, at times heated, and that they must have assumed they were alone. Their conversation swum past his ears in a garbled buzz, with only one word that he could isolate, because both speakers kept repeating it. It was a word unknown to him, but it sounded like *say-me…*

When one of the thinner patches of mist whisked past them, Eddie glimpsed the shapes of the speakers. The man— tall, arms folded and legs planted wide in heavy boots—was wrapped shoulders-to-shins in a heavy cloak. He wore a bandanna over his head, or maybe it was a turban, and something glinted on his ear. The Sea Witch danced and spun as they spoke and appeared to be wearing nothing at all… or something that was barely there. She was not young, nor old, and she moved her voluptuous frame lightly.

The two figures approached each other. Something flashed between them before disappearing into clutched fists.

Eddie and Mr. Higgins, enchanted, peeked over the crates to watch the woman as she resumed her dance, her dark skin shimmering. Was she wearing some sort of sheer, billowing fabric, or was she altogether naked? The fascination of her moving form held them rigid, until there came a sudden gust of cool air. Eddie, still bare-chested, shivered and sneezed.

The conversation on the pier stopped instantly. The tall man looked over in Eddie's direction. The witch stood still. The only sound was the lapping of the waves below them.

"Idiot," whispered the first mate.

Eddie spent a few tense moments debating whether to run away blindly into the fog, whether it was worth the risk of falling off the pier right into the bay.

Then the Sea Witch began to sing her melody again, but this time in English, with an accent peculiar to Eddie's ear. It sounded as if she were singing directly to him, like a serenade:

My ship is made a garden, and my ropes are wrought of vine...

"You had to run around half-naked, didn't you?" the first mate did not bother to whisper.

...when I sing, the fog comes rolling...

Every hair on Eddie's body suddenly stood straight up.

...when I swim, the sea is mine.

Eddie suffered a sharp pain in the back of his head. He fell over, and everything went dark.

Chapter 1
Good with a Knife

He was floating, rolling back and forth, swaying side to side in a boat that was also a crib... Susanna was smiling down at him, humming a sea shanty. She pressed her hand against his forehead and told him he had the fevers. His sweaty head throbbed. She opened a small tin of something to spread on his skin, to help him cool down, and when her hand came into view, it held a squirming mollusk…

Eddie yelled out in fright, waking himself up, and the first thing he saw when he opened his eyes were his own bare legs. With a start, he realized he was naked, lying in a hammock… but it wasn't his hammock on *The Summit of Virtue*. He had no idea where he was, why he was naked, or what had happened to his clothes.

He tried to stay calm. The hammock, he saw, was up against a wall on his right side. When he heaved his left leg over the other side, the hammock began swaying violently. He struggled to stabilize himself but lost his balance and immediately fell four feet to the floor. Only by grabbing a fistful of netting on the way down was he able to right himself and land on his bottom.

The floor felt damp against his sore buttocks. Dazed, he looked back up and saw a crisscross arrangement of six hammocks slung from the walls and corners. They were all empty. In the weak light filtering through the cracks of the wooden walls, Eddie could see no one else in the small barracks, although he could hear gruff voices coming from overhead. On one wall there were rungs to a trapdoor that appeared to be the only way out.

He could recall nothing of what had happened to him, of how he had ended up wherever he was. But as he sniffed the salty air and felt the buckling of the waves beneath him, what he knew for certain was that he was sitting naked in the hull of a ship. And what he could assume from the circumstances was that he had been pressganged. It was exactly what he'd tried to avoid by signing on with Benjamin Williams, whose sterling reputation at Bristol's busy port fed demand for work with his company.

Eddie sighed and hung his head, and immediately noticed that his silver locket had been removed with his clothes. Susanna! He uttered a few choice curses, thinking of whatever else he may never see again, including the knife he'd had on his belt, and his books and other belongings back aboard the *Summit of Virtue*. He refocused his gaze, and the colors of his body accosted him: sun-scorched, freckled arms against sun-starved legs and fish-flesh belly, with ginger hair at his groin—he was a study in shades of red and white. Except his eyes, he knew—as blue as the sky on the summer day you were born, his mother used to tell him—a blue that hadn't changed over his twenty-five years.

Naked or not, he thought, he could try to escape. Maybe the ship wasn't all that far from port yet, or maybe, wherever they were, they were close enough to shore that he could swim the distance. Weighing his options, he decided to climb up the ladder. But he very much desired to cover himself first.

There was a trunk in the corner. He opened it and found it filled with animal hides, of the kind for making leather or parchment. He flipped through them and pulled out the longest he could find, with a span of about four feet.

With a desperate determination, he undid the ties of the lowest hammock. He noticed it was made of a very sturdy cord with a dark purple hue unlike any he'd ever seen. The hammock unloosed, he wound the long hide around his waist, then used the hammock as a belt to bind it. Even though he wrapped it all as tightly as he could, he still felt very exposed. But there was nothing more to do. He knotted the hammock at his hip and ascended only two rungs before he felt the weight of the coverings slipping down his legs. He climbed the rest of the ladder slowly, with one hand holding the makeshift skirt at his hip.

At the top of the rungs, Eddie pushed the trapdoor open a crack, just in time to get splashed in the eyes by someone swabbing the deck. He lowered the door, waited a few moments, and tried again. This time he saw the sailor with the mop, or rather he saw the sailor's bare feet and lower legs. When the sailor walked directly away from him, Eddie eased the door up a little further, and saw that the sailor's skin was a nut-brown color… all over his body.

Eddie let the door close over him, wondering if anyone at all aboard the ship wore clothes, and how they dealt with splinters...

A deep voice called out overhead. "Raintree! Leave the deck for now and go help with the rigging! There's a reef ahead!"

"Aye, cap'n," came the reply, as Eddie spied once again from under the trapdoor. When Raintree dropped the mop and hurried out of sight, Eddie pushed the door open a little further. Just when he thought he would be able to slip onto deck unobserved, his upward force yielded no further movement. Something, or someone, was detaining the door. Eddie looked out through the small space and saw, from underneath, the top of a foot pushing against the door. The foot was missing the fourth and fifth toes.

"The British bloke was quickly woke," a somewhat higher-pitched voice said. "Speak the name you've borne since birth, for this will prove to me your worth."

Eddie felt tempted to lie but decided against it. Whoever was questioning him may well be the captain, and may have already learned his name somehow, in which case the question posed to him was a test of honesty.

"Speak," repeated the man, pushing and releasing his foot impatiently against the door that Eddie still held over his head.

"Eddie Fife, sir."

"Wrong!" called the voice from above, now stamping hard against the trapdoor.

"Wait," yelled Eddie, pulling in his fingers as the door slammed above him. "It's John Edward Fife!"

His shout was met with a prolonged silence, broken finally by the deeper voice he had heard first: "Let him out, Mr. Ola."

The trapdoor opened quickly and completely, blinding Eddie in the sudden bright light. With some trepidation, and attempting to hold his coverings at his waist, he hoisted himself up onto the deck with an awkward lurch. He was kneeling, moving himself into a better position to stand, when the deeper-voiced man yelled out, "Ho! What thing is this upon you? Why are you wrapped... in hammock and hide? My precious hides! I'll charge your own hide for it!"

This man, whom Eddie now assumed to be the captain, roared and lifted his arm to strike him. Eddie scooted backwards on all fours, belly-up, until he ran into Mr. Ola, and the impact made his coverings fall to the deck.

Standing over him, the captain brought down his arm. "Though parts of you are just as red, a crab you are not! Stand! I will strike you as a man!"

Eddie stood, trembling. Covering his crotch with his left hand, he held out his right arm in defense. The captain, just as naked, made no effort to cover any part of himself. Eddie could see he was a tall man of full beard and dark brown skin, broadly muscled, with round scars along his chest.

The captain narrowed his eyes, pursed his mouth, and then burst out laughing. "What is this? What... kind of pernicious shame is come from you? Now I see why you unhooked the hammock and filched the hide. It is because you are ashamed of your body. Deeply so. Which, 'tis the real and much greater shame."

By this point Raintree, Mr. Ola and the rest of the crew, all naked to the wind, had gathered around the captain.

"He is but a lily-livered landlubber," said one.

"I'm no landlubber! I've worked a year and a half with Williams & Sons..."

The same sailor interrupted him. "Ah, but you've a lily liver, still!"

"Don't be so sure," Eddie sputtered.

The captain studied Eddie, who still held his hand to his groin even while standing among so many naked others. "John Edward Fife, look on me well. And look upon all my men, here. We are proud in the heat and the wet, proud to be men, proud to be alive in our bodies. Are you so different from us? What is it you hide—something that makes you so unlike the rest?"

Eddie looked away.

The captain rocked his hips, sending his genitals into a sway. "Well? Is it like or unlike, then?"

Eddie swallowed his embarrassment and tried to sound confident. "It is like."

"If it is nothing outlandish, I say, if your body is merely that of a man, just like the rest of us, then why would we hold any special interest in seeing where you so stubbornly fix our attention? But, by the stars, I'll have you require the use of both hands on this ship, just like the rest of us!"

"Can't I wear... My shirt!" Eddie's gaze focused on the mainsail behind the men, where he had suddenly discerned, in one of its patches, the embroidered monogram design of the linen shirt he had been wearing before the fog rolled in. He began to remember something of the circumstances of his capture but was interrupted.

"Aboard the *Capricorn*, Mr. Fife, there is no wearing of shirts, nor pants, nor boots, nor clothing of any kind! The reasons for such independence from clothing are legion. One of them I think you just discovered: we use any cloth we come by to repair our sails, or for other crafty purposes. But the main reason is that we are men at home in the elements, and we let not the strictures of church nor crown bind us fast!"

Eddie looked at the men, all of them quite dark-skinned, even the blond, blue-eyed man who had insulted him.

"Now," said the captain, "hand me the materials you were using around your waist."

Keeping his left hand between his legs, Eddie scooped up the hammock and the hide from the deck and offered them to the captain.

With a twinkle in his eye, and looking round at his men, the captain continued. "Pick up that mop and scrub the deck."

All eyes upon him, Eddie grabbed the mop with his right hand, and began pushing it with his right arm only, still clutching his penis and scrotum in his left hand.

"Put your back into it!" After passing the hide and hammock to one of his men, the captain posed his hands in the air, as if gripping a mop, and began moving his chest and legs in imitation of the proper way to swab the deck. The men laughed and began imitating their captain. "Harder! Faster!" they all yelled.

Finally Eddie grabbed the mop with both hands, but in the same moment he turned his back to the others, at which they all laughed in a great uproar.

"Well mate, your back end tain't a surprise!"

"Nothing to marvel at! One devil is just like another!"

The captain raised his hand for the men to hush. "Patience, I say. Leave him to his swabbing."

"He'll come 'round the faster without any pester," added Mr. Ola.

The captain turned to him. "Now, Mr. Ola, are we beyond the reef?"

"Aye, sir! Our ship has passed the danger of the reef at last!"

"Continue on course. The rest of you, back to your stations! And you, Mr. Fife—pay me a visit in the captain's quarters once you finish."

The crew dispersed, leaving Eddie to his task. At first, he continued attempting to maneuver the mop with one hand, but he came to realize that he had been left alone, on a ship full of similarly unattired men anyway, and so he soon grabbed the mop with both hands to work much more efficiently. He was angry about it, cursing his conscription and the captain and crew as well, and yet at some point his emotions changed. He felt so free to the breeze, his body wholly thrusting and stretching with his movements, that he found it difficult to stay angry. His spirits lifted in spite of himself, and he finished the deck with a focused satisfaction. Swabbing the deck had never felt so joyful.

He did not need to ask anyone the location of the captain's quarters. The *Capricorn* was a large sloop about seventy feet long, similar in size to the brigantine *Summit of Virtue* and with the same overall layout. He also felt a bit reassured that the *Capricorn* flew no Jolly Roger. There was a flag, but instead of cloth it was a piece of very thin hide, a roughly rectangular stretch of skin. Eddie had heard often enough of buccaneers, who were supposed to hold more honor than pirates, being traders of hides and smoked meats.

He made his way to the stern and knocked on the captain's door.

"Come in," said a voice that Eddie guessed to be Mr. Ola's. He opened the door and saw the captain leaning over a map table. At his side stood Mr. Ola who, as Eddie could see now in comparison, was just as dark as the captain in skin color, though not as tall.

The captain stood, removing his arms from the table, which caused the map to roll up. "Mr. Fife. I see you have regained the free use of both of your hands. I wish to know more about you and your hands. Are you a man of skills?'

Eddie considered the question. "I know how to read and write."

The captain winced. "I suppose that could be of some use."

Eddie quickly mentioned his other known skill. "And I'm good with a knife. A whittler, and a carver, that's me."

At this, the captain raised his eyebrows. "Do you know how to skin a cow? A sheep?"

"No sir, that's a thing I've never done. But I am a swift apprentice."

The captain's eyes narrowed. He turned and had a brief conversation with Mr. Ola in a language Eddie did not understand. While they spoke, Eddie scanned the contents of the captain's quarters: his hammock in a corner, a couple of chests on the floor, a rack with several bottles that were probably full of rum, some fruit on the table, some built-in shelves with books and scrolls, a spyglass, a compass, and a few other odds and ends, and a large sword in its sheath that hung from a peg. Most curious were the half dozen angular wooden masks affixed to the walls. Of different sizes and expressions, they all had wide holes for eyes and even wider ones for mouths.

Then the captain stood to his full height, about a head taller than Eddie, and approached him. "Have you no recollection of me?"

Eddie stared blankly. "No, sir."

"I shall jog your memory," said the captain, and with that he began to hum a haunting tune that seemed familiar.

As light glinted from the ring in the captain's ear, images popped quickly into Eddie's mind: the fog, the crates, the dancing woman…

"You… it was you on the pier in Cartagena. You spoke with the Sea Witch."

The captain smiled. "Aye. Is that what you call her? 'Tis true, that. She is indeed a witch of the sea."

Eddie made a respectful nod and addressed himself to Mr. Ola. "Sir, how did you know my full name?"

"You left your name slung over a rail, now it hangs from the middle of the sail," Mr. Ola replied.

Eddie remembered the monogram on his shirt—the initials JEF that Susanna had embroidered for him—and understood that Mr. Ola had guessed his first initial to stand for John, a common enough name. He blushed, aware he was turning an even darker red than usual on his face and chest.

"No need for shame," said the captain. "I take your question as a good sign. You are already forgetting your clothes."

Eddie nodded but hesitated a moment. "And cap'n sir, what is your name?"

The tall, dark man gave him a piercing look. "Call me Captain Barlo."

"Captain Barlo, sir, why… why did you kidnap me?"

The man's smile withered into a scowl. "I thought we were on friendlier terms, lad. I did not kidnap you. I rescued you… from the Sea Witch."

Eddie looked to the captain's companion, as if to verify this assertion, but received only a stony stare. "On the pier, I was with another man, a Mr. Higgins, the first mate from the *Summit of Virtue*. Was he not... rescued as well?"

The two exchanged a glance, and it was Mr. Ola who spoke. "Boy, you are the luckier of the pair. Your first mate… vanished into the air."

"I see," Eddie said with a gulp. "Sirs, uh… also, if I may be so bold, when you confiscated my clothes, did you secret away, uh, some of my other belongings?"

"Aye," said the captain. "You see, when we *rescued* you," he emphasized, "we found it necessary to disarm you of weapons, amulets, anything you might have tried to use against us. You might have harmed, unwittingly, your very rescuers." He opened a drawer in his table and pulled out a silver locket on a chain, and a knife, and indicated with a nod that Eddie could retrieve them.

Eddie recognized them instantly and began to put his locket back around his neck.

"You haven't asked," began the captain, "but I shall inform you that the wearing of lockets, medallions, earrings, and other such decorative items is indeed permitted aboard the *Capricorn* at my discretion."

"Understood," Eddie nodded. "May I have your permission to wear the locket, sir?"

"Answer for me, first," replied Captain Barlo, "who t'was who gave you her lovely silver heart?"

Eddie cringed in the realization that he should have anticipated the question.

The captain smiled broadly. "Isn't there an inscription inside the locket, Mr. Ola? In verse, no?"

"No, captain, not verse," replied the first mate. "In fact it's quite terse: *Unto...*"

"Cease! Let us hear Mr. Fife recite the inscription. Otherwise, how do we know he didn't steal the locket from someone else? So," prodded the captain. "What does it say?"

Eddie knew the phrase, of course. *"Unto thine heart keep me bound, S."*

Mr. Ola nodded to the captain that this was correct. "Who is S, then?" Barlo wanted to know.

Eddie considered making up a name, but desisted, if only because he did not quite trust nor understand the explanation of what had happened to Mr. Higgins. The *Summit of Virtue* first mate could have been interrogated and would have known the answer to the captain's question.

"Susanna, sir. Susanna Hemsworth."

"Susanna Hemsworth," Barlo repeated, pondering the information, and Eddie bore the shock of hearing the name of his beloved uttered carelessly from this stranger's lips, so far away from home and at so inopportune a moment.

"Very good," the captain continued. "And does she live anywhere close to here?"

"She lives in Bristol, sir, in England. We've known each other since we were children. Sir."

"How quaint! Mr. Ola, here, is the only person left to me that I've known since childhood. The rest of our hometown was… evacuated."

The captain stroked his beard, contemplating Mr. Fife. "You may don the locket," he said finally. "'Tis not my place to offer you any counsel other than what is oft said, and what in your case will no doubt be true: There are many fish in the sea."

Eddie's blank stare, as his fingers fumbled with the locket clasp, was met with knowing chuckles from the other two men.

"Now," said the captain, "let's see what you can do with that knife. Mr. Ola, pass him that stick of driftwood from the shelf."

Clearing his throat and setting his jaw, Mr. Ola first produced his own knife from a sheath on a thin leather belt, the only item he was wearing. He tossed the blade in his hand a few times, expertly, with his eyes on Eddie. Then he gave him the small log about the length of his forearm, with a warning: "Act with strife, and you'll lose your life."

Mr. Ola punctuated this point with an effective demonstration, hurling his knife into a guava from the table that the captain had tossed straight up into the air casually but on cue. The bright yellow guava flew to the cabin wall and stuck fast, right into the gaping mouth of one of the wooden masks, with droplets of pink juice oozing from its puncture.

Eddie swallowed hard, nodding. He began turning the piece of wood in his hands, rubbing and pressing to sense its heft and texture, and an idea came to him. He judged it soft and small enough to make a good show of his craft. Knife in hand, he got to work. The other men watched him at first, but then returned to their discussion over the map.

"It couldn't be east of Saint-Domingue," Eddie heard the captain say before the two men switched back to their language.

After a quarter of an hour, Eddie stopped whittling and placed his finished product on the table.

The captain picked it up and scoffed. "A toy boat?"

"It has several particulars," Eddie said. "It's flat on the bottom, see? You can place round objects in there, like those guavas, to keep them from rolling around your table as the ship tilts. You can also use it to hold down the edge of your map, there."

Both men looked at Eddie with raised eyebrows.

"I can polish it up some more, if you'd like…"

"No need," said the captain. "It is enough to know your skills."

"John Edward Fife is good with a knife," quipped Mr. Ola.

"Indeed," responded Barlo. "Now, we'll make a better use for your skills. Go find Raintree and tell him I said to teach you how to skin a goat."

Chapter 2
Skinners

After he left the captain's quarters, Eddie passed a man who looked to be from East Asia, very heavily tattooed all over his body. The man was seated on a barrel, sewing, of all things, a bright red military jacket with deep blue epaulets. The jacket had been cut in two, right down the middle of the back, and the man was sewing it back together, though very loosely. Matching pants had been folded neatly on the barrel next to him. The man stopped his work to look at Eddie.

"New man. Do you miss your clothes now?"

"Aye, I think I'm still missing them a bit. But why are you mending yours?"

The other man laughed. "These no mine. The captain use these… on special occasion."

"I see," said Eddie, who was sure he didn't really understand. "But your clothes… your clothes are your tattoos, right?"

The man set the jacket down in his lap and extended his arms to his sides, showing Eddie more of his markings. "Wearing nothing but tattoos is like… being clothed and being naked at the same time."

Eddie was about to ask what a particular spiral tattoo on the man's shoulder meant, but didn't want to be too personal.

The tattooed sailor guessed his intention. "I am Antonio. I tell you all about my tattoos some other time. We get back to our work now, yes?"

Eddie nodded and continued on his way.

He found Raintree in the galley, a slaughtered beast at his feet. Fresh blood colored the man's legs, hands, and forearms, with further crimson splotches on other areas of his anatomy.

"I see the cap'n gave yer knife back," said Raintree. "Are ya gonna help, or are ya gonna just stand there with yer teeth in yer mouth?"

"He says you're to show me how to skin."

"Oh, he does, does he? Well of course he does. Seeing as how ya can't be a proper skinner without ya know how to skin a animal. But that's only the first step, mind, because then you have to learn the scraping, and the salting, and the soaking… and the tanning…"

"You know what you're about. I'll be sure to learn it from you."

The older man had squatted close to the carcass, and he looked up at Eddie. "Come on, then, you've got to get down close, here, and watch what I'm doing."

Raintree clutched one of the goat's hind legs just above the hoof and began to slit the skin up toward the tail. Then he passed the leg to Eddie for him to finish. "Once you get up to the belly, be very careful or you'll slice the bowels right open, and I'll wager you know what would happen then."

Eddie, still overly conscious of his nudity, of kneeling opposite another naked man with a bloody carcass between them, tried to concentrate on slicing and sawing cleanly.

"We'd have shite all over our supper, that's what would happen then!" Raintree snorted. "But I can see yer doing it right. You know yer way with a knife... Could be useful for a time."

When he felt like he could talk while still focusing on the goatskin, Eddie asked Raintree if he knew where they were headed.

"Aye, and I suppose there's no harm in tellin' ya. We be headed straight north, into the open sea, Jamaica-bound."

Eddie kept his eyes on the goat and betrayed no surprise, although he had assumed they would be staying closer to shore.

Raintree was watching him intently. "Ya said ya been working for a trading company for more than a year, didn' ya? Well at least yer familiar with the life at sea. Just not so used to nekkid, eh?"

Eddie stopped slicing a moment to look at this man, who was probably two score or more years older than he, with deeply tanned skin, a greying beard, and the tentacles of a tattooed octopus sprawling across his chest. "I'm getting used to it. I guess I can say that naked's practical… except maybe splinters. But you must admit it's odd, no? I mean, how did you get used to being a naked sailor?"

The older man chuckled. "Oh, I were used to it already. I learnt right quick that I didn't need no garb. That's about the first thing ya learn when yer a castaway."

"You were a castaway?" In surprise, Eddie almost sliced too deep into the goat's abdomen.

"Mind what yer doin' there! Aye, 'twas a Dutch ship what attacked us. I was sailing with Drysdale at the time. We were low on ammunition, and once we ran out, it was every man for hisself. How many perished, only the fishes could tell, but I managed to wash ashore with breath in my chest."

"How did you survive?"

"Lucky for me, I ended up on a wee islet with plenty of palm trees. Persisted on coconuts and rainwater, I did, and what fish or lizards I could catch. 'Twas lonely and rough, and me clothes fell to tatters. Those rags were more useful for gettin' a fire started than for coverin' me body. Eventually fortune smiled on me again, because one afternoon I got a fire going just as a ship was coming by. It was the very ship we're on right now, the *Capricorn*. Cap'n Barlo saw the smoke and pulled the ship close and sent in Mr. Ola on a rowboat. I was so accustomed to me own skin, 'twere no surprise to me at all to see him nekkid too… Ya know, sittin' here gabbin' with ya now, it's only if I put my mind to it that I can remember what it was like back in the day, to be bindin' meself up in garments all the while. Don't miss it, that's fer sure."

As Raintree spoke, Eddie finished freeing the goat's hide from all four legs. Then the older man took over, bidding Eddie watch him.

"Pay attention to what I'm doing here while you tell me where yer from and what kind of man ya are."

Eddie sat back and stretched his legs. "I'm from Bristol. I'm the third of six in my family: four sons and two daughters, all of us red-haired and fair-skinned, but it's only me out of all of us Fifes who learned his letters. My papa allowed me to read what books I could find, but mostly I'd write down the stories I heard, especially stories of the sea, like the defeat of the Spanish Armada, the adventures of Sinbad the Sailor, the exploits of Sir Walter Raleigh, and the perils of Ulysses."

Raintree snorted. "I'ent heard o' none of 'em save Raleigh."

"Well they're all good tales. And listening to them, and then writing them down, I built up quite a fancy for what I hoped would be my life at sea, even though I knew there would be hard work in store. Plenty of old salts in Bristol— the same ones who'd sing the old sea shanties—they made sure I learned that dangers like scurvy are far more common than sea monsters, or cyclops, or Circe."

"What? Circe?"

"She was a sea witch... Huh! Maybe sea witches are more common than I thought."

"I'ent believe in witches," Raintree stated. Then he muttered on for a while, lost in his own musings, yet practiced enough to keep slicing the hide clean away.

Eddie looked around the galley, noticing a ray of sunlight streaming through the door and falling across his bare legs. "But, I can tell you, even on the sunniest, brightest days in Bristol, I never thought of being naked at sea. How would I have imagined it, if I had never read nor heard of such a thing? Nobody tells tales or sings songs of naked sailors… And so there I was on the *Summit of Virtue*, not thinking much about clothing, just taking it for granted that everybody wears clothes. But now, I've discovered a precious truth. Life can be otherwise." He closed his eyes, feeling the health, the hearth of the sun inside him, as if by opening his skin to the sky, he had become a host for the light within him. He could feel already that he had become a sunnier, brighter man.

"Hey there, Fife, keep yer eyes open! I be learnin' ya still!" Eddie sat forward and paid attention to the rest of the procedure, which, just as they were removing the tripe, was interrupted by Mr. Ola.

"Hold!" yelled the first mate, hobbling quickly into the galley while waving something about in his hand. "I give you the one half part of a sphere. Now please, you place all the entrails in here!"

"Oh fer cryin' in the bloody soup, man," cried Raintree. "Ya scared me clear to the threshold o' death, ya did. Here, Fife, scoop all that in there."

Fife did as he was told, noting the brightly colored spiral painted inside the wooden vessel that Mr. Ola clutched. The first mate, with a wild look in his eyes and a rough breath from his chest, thanked him and then squatted on the floor, placing the bowl between his legs.

"I should have remembered, shouldn't I? He told me he was gonna be needin' the tripe," grumbled Raintree. "Beyond me what he does with it."

Under Raintree's supervision, Eddie began slicing meat from the bone, but his concentration was impeded by the interjections and utterances coming from the corner where Mr. Ola sat, sifting through the bowl:

"Very dry…" spoke the first mate to himself. "What is this seed? This is unknown anywhere west of Lisbon..."

Eddie looked over just in time to see the man bring the seed to his face, sniff it, and lick it. Eddie grimaced, but Mr. Ola merely kept on pulling items out of the bowl and holding them up to inspect.

"A goat will eat anything," Raintree whispered.

Mr. Ola huffed loudly. "In the belly of the goat, the portents of the world are wrote. Look here, Raintree," he said, holding high a wooden button. "This tells me that the season of the hurricane has not yet begun."

Raintree chuckled. "Really, now? You can divine the weather from what a goat ate off a clothesline?"

"Indeed. He who would see, let him look. He who would eat, let him cook," replied the first mate, waving his hand for Raintree to attend to his own labors.

Eddie went back to slicing, although he'd spy a look from time to time to see the items that Mr. Ola extracted and lined up in front of him on the galley floor with the button and the seed: a damaged cork, a thimble, a lump of wax, some twine, a few pieces of eight, and something that might have been part of a bone. When the first mate gasped loudly, Eddie looked to see him holding up a cowrie shell. Mr. Ola polished it with some spit, tossed it a few times in his hand, and set the bowl aside. Using the twine, he laid out a circle on the floor, and set the other objects around it like a wreath. Then he closed his eyes, uttered an incantation in his language, and tossed the cowrie like a die in the middle of the circle.

The cowrie shell landed with the open side up. Mr. Ola raised his chin high and clenched his fists. Before Eddie could tell what was happening, the first mate was standing over him, clutching his shoulders and staring at his locket. Then Mr. Ola suddenly grasped Eddie's chin and stared into his face. "We have chosen well. That man is wise who opens his eyes."

He placed his right hand on Eddie's head for a moment, then left the galley.

Eddie felt goosebumps rise on his arms, and didn't know if it was a good sign, or a bad sign, or what exactly any of it had to do with him.

Raintree shrugged his shoulders. "He's a mysterious fellow. But the cap'n must keep him around for some reason, don't you think?"

"I don't know *what* to think."

"Then let's not think about it at all," suggested Raintree, and the two of them got back to work. Eddie followed the cook's guidance, from scraping off the fat for tallow, all the way up through getting the goat meat stew cooking over the tin firebox. Only after the flames were steady did Raintree offer him some wash water to clean off the goat blood. When Eddie learned the stew would fill the stomachs of the entire crew, and not just the officers as would have been the case aboard the *Summit of Virtue*, he smiled so broadly that Raintree was moved to curse the British and all the awful victuals he'd ever had the misfortune of tasting in London.

The stew simmered long through the day while Eddie and the rest of the men busied themselves with their tasks under a sunny sky. When it was finally time for mess, the crew all stood around a long table that unfolded from a wall, each of the dozen sailors resting his arms on either side of his plate to keep it from sliding onto the floor as the ship rolled. The captain ate with them; only one man stayed on deck to keep a lookout.

Captain Barlo licked his lips. "How long do you think this stew will do us, Raintree?"

"I'd reckon at least another day, Cap'n."

"A good enough spell."

When the men had finished, the captain smiled benevolently and passed around some bottles of rum. "You there, James Clayton, take us up on deck for a song," he said. "We're celebrating the very timely arrival—very timely indeed—of this gentleman here, Mr. Fife, who seems to have finally forgotten his garb."

After a rowdy toast, Raintree let the men know that Eddie had never heard a tale of naked sailors.

"Yer a'gonna hear one now!" yelled James Clayton, jumping up to fetch his fiddle. The men cheered and moved up on deck.

James Clayton was the sailor who had angrily called Eddie a lily-livered landlubber when he'd first come up on deck, but now, in anticipation of singing, he was all grace and charm. "This is a ballad we'll dedicate to Mr. Fife," he called out, leading into the tune on his fiddle. "'The Tale of the Mermaids Three.'"

"I know this one…" Eddie started to say, but he was quickly hushed.

"*A long time ago on the open sea,*" began James Clayton, and Eddie anticipated the rest of the first verse:

when I was just a young lad,
my grandpa to me sung had
the tale of the mermaids three.

It was a melody Eddie knew by heart, with its jaunty stress on the words *young* and *sung*. Under his breath, he began singing along with James Clayton on the next verse:

As handsome and hale as a man could wish,
like sisters were the mermaids,
each beauty fash'ning her braids,
top woman, and bottom fish.

Even though he was a little disappointed to hear a song he already knew, Eddie could admit that James Clayton was both a fine tenor and an accomplished fiddler. But since the other men were singing along too, especially Mr. Ola, Eddie lifted his voice and continued with them:

They lived in a cove on an island wee
and sang to while the day long.
Of sea shanties and gay songs
they knew every melody.

But some of their songs cast a magic spell -
to change the weather, they would.
To call the creatures, they could -
the fishes both fair and fell.

Just as Eddie began to sing the next words, he stopped. James Clayton's version was no longer the same as what he had learned. With great attention and curiosity, he listened as the singers carried on:

On a night of no wind when the moon was gone,
a ship stole into their bay.
Its captain called to there lay
the anchor to hold them drawn.

SKINNERS

His voice carried far on the waters still.
The mermaids learned of their goal
to steal the pearls from their shoal,
and their many coffers fill.

"Attack!" yelled the sirens, with swishing tails.
The palms, bewitched, bent downward
like cannons facing outward,
and shot coconuts toward sails.

From far, far away on a magic gale
flew onions, garlic, lemons,
potatoes, carrots, peppers
to fall in the bay like hail.

The three hexed the bay like a boiling pot
and stirred the food together.
"What is this awful weather?"
"We're cooked, sir! The stew is hot!"

The men on the ship stripped their waistcoats off.
Their pants and boots and shirtsleeves
dropped on the deck like birch leaves.
All cov'rings were promptly doffed.

Then steaming and sweating and sore afraid
they called for help most loudly.
The captain to his crowd, he
yelled, "Hold, men! We've been waylaid!"

But the mermaids did pity the sailors nude
and split legs from their fishtails,
and truce flags from rent ship sails,
to take to the men some food.

"Eat," said the sisters, and served the stew.
Then they all downed their supper,
not missing any cover,
the mermaids, the cap'n, or crew.

"Now dance," said the mermaids, and dance they did.
All thoughts of theft had vanished.
Since clothing had been banished,
of ill plans they all were rid.

And this is the secret, dear list'ners true:
When you remove your clothing,
your life will lack for no thing
and hold greater pleasure, too.

The men repeated the last verse, lifting their mugs of rum on high.

"There ya have it, Fife!" roared Raintree, a spirited flush on his cheeks. "A song of naked sailors!"

Eddie smiled, nodding his head in agreement. "I thought I knew that one, but it had a different ending."

"Right, right," said James Clayton, pulling on his beard. "I bet you know the one where the mermaids save the city from a pirate attack. Ho hum. Listen, laddie, seeing as how we's skinners, and by that I mean awfully close to pirates, don't you reckon we'd go for a different story?"

"'Twere better for the pirates to join the mermaids," said Raintree.

"Aye," Mr. Ola agreed, "better for the skinners to join the finners."

"*Aiwa*, join," yelled Jabari, unsteady on his feet. He was a large man who looked to be of Mediterranean origin. "I like sing dance join mermaids!"

Captain Barlo was watching Eddie with a curious gleam in his eye. "And you, Mr. Fife… what do you think of mermaids?"

Eddie returned his gaze uncertainly. "What do you mean, sir?"

"Do you believe in them?"

"I don't know, sir. I've never seen one." Eddie looked around the deck at the crew. "Dancing with mermaids. Everybody bare. I think… it's a wonder, a beautiful fantasy." He sighed. "Are there any more songs about naked sailors?"

The men looked down at the deck or out to the horizon, suddenly quiet.

"Naked… at sea… anything?"

Someone started to whistle halfheartedly. Captain Barlo strode away toward his quarters. Eddie figured the crew had exhausted their repertoire with the one song.

Several hours later, however, Eddie had heard the men sing through "The Naked Navy of Norway," "The Ballad of Castaway Carlos," "Neptune's Nymph Chorale," "The Isle of Paradise Found," and quite a few others, including the ballad of Fair Helga, a nude figurehead who sprang to life from the prow of her Viking ship to vanquish a sea serpent.

"Really," Eddie said at last, struggling to stay awake. "Truly. Marvelous. Who knew there could be so many songs about… naked…?"

James Clayton, who by that point was lying face-up on the deck, still humming to the stars, called out: "We'll pick up with the rest of the tunes tomorrow, mates!"

Chapter 3
Skin Stories

When he awoke the next morning, Eddie needed a few moments to remember his new whereabouts: the naked ship. Unclothed as he was in his hammock, surrounded by four unclothed crewmates sleeping in theirs (Antonio, Mr. Ola, James Clayton and Jabari; Raintree was on watch), he mused that living without clothing all the time still took some getting used to. But aside from that stark difference, the *Capricorn* was a vessel not unlike the *Summit of Virtue*. Even though she showed her age more than the merchant ship—Eddie heard it in the creaking of her planks, he smelled it in her musty underbelly, he could see it in the patched-up sails—it was easy for him to fall into a shipboard maintenance routine very similar to what he had been accustomed to before. The rigging, the sails, the deck—all of the *Capricorn* was familiar to him by that point. Captain Barlo's ship did have a smaller crew, though, and so Eddie, because of his knife skills, became very useful to Raintree in the galley, where he helped with everything from slicing turnips to gutting groupers. In turn, Raintree helped him use some scrap hide to fashion a belt with a sheath for his knife. The leather belt chafed against Eddie's bare hips at first, but before long he became used to it.

The most fundamental difference aboard Barlo's ship, however, was the daily application of a kind of ointment that the sailors called sunskin. Naked under the sun all day, the crew had a strong need to protect their skin. All the men used sunskin, even the captain, regardless of how dark their skin was naturally. Sunskin did not smell exactly pleasant, nor wholly unpleasant. Eddie could only guess its ingredients. According to Raintree, the production of the ointment was managed in secret, and Captain Barlo bartered for it at great cost. It was the solemn duty of the sailors to apply it individually on a daily basis, from head to toe and every little spot in between, and to mutually help apply it to each other's backs. Anyone who ended up with a burnt back had the option, though rarely employed, of lashing the man who had been stingy with sunskin that day. As he began to use it, Eddie noticed that not only was he able to avoid sunburn, but also his skin seemed healthier than ever before—smoother, less itchy—even as it slowly darkened to a shade that he had never experienced on his fair and freckled self.

Eddie felt a twinge of hesitation that morning, the first time he had to apply the sunskin to a crew-mate's back. He could already understand everyone's need for it, as well as the unavoidable fact that no one can reach his own back, yet he had never touched another man in that way, or for such an odd mixed motive of health and camaraderie. He didn't want to appear to be touching the other man's back for too long, but he knew he had to apply the sunskin thoroughly for his mate or face the consequences. So he gained a new anatomical appreciation for the neck, the shoulder blades, the ribs, and all the vast plateau of the back—in particular, Jabari's. Jabari, who Eddie learned hailed from Egypt, was very tall, with a very broad back. Eddie understood that as the rookie, he had been allotted the "extra" work.

It wasn't that Eddie had never noticed the structure and variety of the male torso before. On the *Summit of Virtue*, the crew had worked bare-chested on occasion, and Eddie had seen his share of scrunched shoulders, bunched-up chest muscles, and expansive abdomens in action. Yet on Barlo's ship, he felt not only a greater freedom from clothes, of course, but also a greater comfort with his own body and among the bodies of others. This comfort led to a more nuanced scrutiny of anatomy through the familiarity of daily routine, a license to notice bodies and how they work. He observed, for example, the parallel pulling of arms and thighs among the men weighing anchor, the minor movement of nipples back and forth over the chests of sailors who were counting out lengths of rope, and the meridians traced head to toe by freely flowing sweat. The strong odors of working men, he realized, were quickly diminished by the breeze when there was no clothing to trap them. He grew to understand the buttocks as a pair of hinges not unlike the elbows or knees, but with greater padding, and he marveled, discreetly, that the attitudes of the flaccid penis depend not only on a given man's particular anatomy but also on the heat, the breeze, the humidity, and even the time of day. Eddie noticed all these details as an earnest student of experience with a noble heart, and if he thought about them, he understood that he was justifying, through these physiological observations, the appreciation that was growing within him for being naked.

It was an appreciation that he felt full force when a front passed through on the afternoon of his third day on board.

"It's a squall!" came Clayton's cry, as the sky darkened and the waves stirred high all around them.

"Batten the hatches!" roared Barlo, and the men began preparing for the sudden downpour.

In a matter of minutes, Eddie felt the wet wind encounter his skin from every conceivable direction, and the shocks of rain and wave were no less innovative and unpredictable in the angles from which they splashed his body. It felt exhilarating. Aboard the old mercantile ship, he would have suffered his wet clothes clinging to him during the storm, and for a long time afterward as well, while they slowly and unevenly dried out. But here on the *Capricorn*, as the fury of the tempest abated, Eddie and the other men were dry in no time, from head to toe. No chills, no shivering, no damp crotch, no itching buttocks!

Eddie also discovered that his fellow shipmates proved extremely easy to talk with, and he began to wonder if the communal nudity caused such frankness. Everyone, except for the more reserved Captain Barlo and Mr. Ola, spoke easily of their past, their loved ones, and their hopes, and even sought out the opportunity to do so. These conversations happened whether swabbing the deck, manning the sails, eating, or lying in the hammocks at night.

This openness of character was so absolute that Eddie came to observe something he had only ever heard about: a romantic relationship between men. James Clayton would often hold hands with Antonio, and they could even be seen to kiss from time to time. In spite of the hateful and disparaging remarks about such men that Eddie had heard growing up in Bristol, where such a relationship would have been seen as an intolerable aberration, these two lovers were robust in appearance, noble of heart, and the love they shared seemed genuine. No one on board begrudged them their relationship. When Antonio, with his dark hair and complexion and his many tattoos, would stand next to the paler, blond and tattoo-less James Clayton, with their arms around each other as they looked out to sea, the contrasting colors of their skin and hair fascinated Eddie.

"Stare not, Fife," intoned Captain Barlo on one such occasion. "The body is a magnificent marvel, but not for this do we gape and gawk."

"Excuse me, Captain," said Eddie, startled, forcing himself to look down at the deck.

"Those two enjoy a union that is unique to them," the captain continued. "Unlike the rest of us, who miss our loved ones far away, they have each other to hold, right on board this ship. But the challenge is that they do not have much space or time to share together. So, just because they can be seen, does not mean they are inviting your contemplation."

"I understand, Captain," replied Eddie.

Captain Barlo began to walk away, and Eddie noticed for the first time the long scar running almost vertically along his back, a deep mark that must have been left by a whip. Eddie dared attempt to detain him with a question.

"Captain, where are we?"

He replied without turning around. "In the middle of the sea."

Eddie sighed. "Aye, Captain."

Then the captain spun on his heel. "Do you have a particular reason to know where we are, more precisely?"

"No, sir."

"Good. Then let me tell you where we are, more generally. I shall locate you, since you seem in need of orientation. Here in the great bowl of this sea we come to mix—we, the wayward peoples of other lands, all tossed and washed together in this same basin. And we are blessed to mingle here, where there is nothing so fresh as the fish, the fruit, the flowers. Here in the Caribbean, the ill-fitting nationalities and religions of old—the strictures and restrictions of all kinds—they wear thin, and threadbare, and fall off like old breeches. Here, Fife, you can be free, in ways that I suspect you have not imagined to exist. Freedom, Fife! Will you understand? This New World… this is freedom."

Captain Barlo stretched his arms to the sky in emphasis. But he lowered them slowly and looked again at Eddie.

"With freedom, of course, comes responsibility. You do indeed have duties to me as long as you remain aboard the *Capricorn*. Should you tire of such commitment, we will negotiate your ability to search out your freedom elsewhere."

"Aye, Captain."

Raintree appeared at that moment, carrying a wet mass dripping down his legs. "Here, Fife, come attend on a racking." He raised his hands and nodded toward the wet lump. "'Tis the hide what we skinned from the goat three days ago. I been soakin' it in a barrel o' seawater."

"Indeed," affirmed Barlo. "Look to this matter, sailor."

It was well known around the Caribbean that hides were in high demand. The captain and his crew used them to barter for just about everything they needed, from food to weapons to supplies, including sunskin. Eddie had learned that Barlo and his skinners maintained a home base of sorts on one of the islands, where an associate tended goats and a few sheep and cattle. The associate received a cut of the profits because he did most of the skinning, tanning and related work to produce the hides.

"We'll be needin' yer knife," Raintree advised, "but first help me get the frame fixed."

He set the soaked hide down on the deck and began untying a frame that had been secured against the outer wall of the galley. Eddie helped undo the knots, and then they carried the frame over to a pair of posts outside the captain's quarters. Each post had two tight shackles, one above and one below. Eddie had noticed the posts some days earlier, imagining they had some awful punitive function, perhaps for flogging. But he saw now that the large frame fit snugly into the shackles to hold each corner tight, exposing both sides of the frame to the sun and air. Once the frame was in place, Raintree showed him how to puncture the hide along the edges, every few inches, so they could stretch it taut with cord tied to the frame.

"Punch them holes a little further in,' said Raintree, "and when ya goes to pull the cord, mind ya don't be rippin' the edges o' the hide."

The process was just quick and new enough for Eddie to avoid tedium, although it did take longer than he thought it would to center the hide. As he drew another cord tight around the frame, he imagined carving designs onto the supple skin. He wondered about the size of the frame. "Is this big enough for cowhide?"

"Fer a calf, I reckon, but not a full cow, no sirree. Paco—that's our man back on Cuba—he's got much larger frames fer that. But we help on board with what we can. This frame'll do fer goats, an' sheep, an' also sharks."

"Sharks?"

"Aye. Different procedure fer sharks, though. And 'gators."

Eddie listened with interest to Raintree's instructions for the tanning process— "We'll hafta do that on the morn'! Those brains are a-stewin'"—interspersed with a story about a pirate who killed his brother over a very fine pair of sharkskin boots.

"The boots had a design what, if ya knew how to read it, showed the way to a buried treasure," explained Raintree, "and the brother found out how to read it. But to anybody else they just looked like a pair of leather-crafted boots with some shapes etched into 'em. I saw 'em meself."

"A treasure map hidden in plain sight," marveled Eddie.

"That it was," mused Raintree, who took a step back to inspect their work and noticed that Antonio walked by behind the frame. His eye moved from the hide to Antonio. "In fact," said the cook, "there was a mark on them boots what looked like that one there on Antonio's shoulder."

Antonio stopped and pointed at the top of his left arm, where there was a spiral around a cluster of dots, with the largest dot in the center. "This one?"

"That be the one," replied Raintree. "What's it fer?"

"Is shows me connected to me family, me people," replied Antonio. "And is shows we connected to the stars."

Raintree scowled. "No buried treasure?"

Antonio thought for a moment, then pointed to his heart. "Yes, the buried treasure is here. Is where my family lives."

Raintree blew a raspberry. "Go round once again on each knot, Fife, tight as ya can make it, eh? Then come to the galley so's I can show ya how we're gonna finish the brains for tannin'."

As the older man started to walk away, Antonio asked him, "What about yours? What mean?"

"Ah, the octopus?" Raintree turned his chest to show how its deep purple tentacles unfurled across his left side. "Ta be honest, it ain't no treasure map neither. It's just because I like 'em, octopuses. I like how they look, I like how they swim, I even like how they taste."

"As good as reason," said Antonio.

Raintree headed to the galley, and Antonio was about to leave as well, but Eddie asked him if he could explain his other tattoos.

Antonio hesitated for a moment. "I no tell me skin stories, but I know you quite curious since the other day. In that case I no mind. I give you short versions. See these lines down me arms and legs? They mean strength and… how you say? Force of life. From me father and me grandfathers."

Eddie let go of the cord he had pulled, changing his focus from the skin of the goat to the skin of his crewmate. "What are the ones that go down your back, like angled waves?"

"Yes, those lightning bolts. They soul, they what brings we to life."

There were twinned circles on Antonio's buttocks and calves that matched the ones centered over his nipples. Eddie pointed them out. "And these?"

"They also force of life, but from me mother and me grandmothers. And another circle, here around me neck."

44

Antonio indicated broad bands flowing front and back over his shoulders that looked like a heavy necklace or a collar. "This circle, uh… the… opening of me mother. It remind me that I born into this world just like anyone else. But it also to honor the head and what treasure it holds: me thoughts, plans, dreams, memories."

"I like that, but I wonder, doesn't it hurt?"

"No. It does not now. Maybe you mean when I had them put onto me? Yes, that hurted. A lot. It hurted more in some areas, like the neck, than on the legs. When it happening, you have to be strong. Some people take a special drink, a tea, to numb the pain. I did not."

"Do you think I could get one?"

Antonio smiled. "Yes. I know someone can do it the next time you in Santo Domingo. There may be others, but none do it just like back on the Visayas. That's me home. When the Spaniards came they called us *pintados,* painted people."

Eddie gave a slight nod and went back to pulling cords on the goatskin. Antonio observed him a moment.

"What skin story would you tell, Fife? Where would you put on your body?"

Eddie smiled. "I've got a while to think about it, don't I?"

As Antonio left him, Eddie's mind went back to imagining shapes on the goatskin, and what they might look like on his own skin. Would he make a likeness of Susanna? It would be easier to design the letters of her name over a heart… But the nagging doubt came to him: would he ever see her again? As he walked into the galley to learn from Raintree how they were going to tan the hide, he couldn't release the thought that Captain Barlo had not an ounce of sympathy for his longing for Susanna, and he would never be able to return to her without some sort of negotiation… or drastic action.

***

That evening, Eddie decided to approach the captain. "Sir, a word if I may."

"You may, Fife. What, you're missing those clothes?"

"No sir. I'm missing my lady, Susanna. What say you, can we strike a bargain?"

"You miss your miss?" Barlo gave a wry chuckle. "You are not in a very good position to bargain. And yet, in such high esteem you hold her! How would you match her price?"

Eddie had anticipated this, had been mulling it over all afternoon. "Port Royal, sir. If I can but get there, I can place a loan through Williams & Company. I…"

The captain's gales of laughter interrupted him. "Port Royal! A nest of vipers. How would you have me place my trust on what may or may not happen in Port Royal, where one can't even trust water to run downhill?"

"Spanish Town, then. Wherever I can find a representative. Sir, you must give me a chance!"

The captain scowled. "No. I am under no obligation to give you any chance whatsoever. And if your offer is a dodgy loan through your former employ, then you have no exchange worth considering."

Eddie hesitated just a moment. "Have you never loved?"

Barlo drew his right hand up so quickly that Eddie flinched, raising his arm in defense of an imminent blow. But the captain's hand continued upward, to the darkening sky.

46

"Love," he thundered. "Love! Aye, deeply have I loved, and mightily, as one should! With all the heart, and bones, and all the fire within!" He paused and brought his arm down. "But it did not last, Fife. Love never lasts. One does not yoke one's heart to another like a pair of oxen. That silver heart you wear—that is the only kind of heart that will last, long after your bones have crumbled."

"But sir, you can love again."

The captain smiled. "Then you have made my case for me."

Eddie lowered his head.

"I will speak no more of this, sailor. What I will say is that you would be better served to keep your heart, and your head, right here, where your body is now, not back in Bristol."

"I will return there. Someday, somehow."

The captain grabbed Eddie's shoulders and gave him a shake. "Listen to me, Fife. My crew and I, we have a business to run, a reputation to protect. We are the original skinners, the naked buccaneers. We are your employ now."

"I'm merely a pair of arms to you. What matter whether it be me or someone else? At Port… at any port we make, we can find a sailor to replace…"

The captain cut him off. "Mr. Ola believes you will be suitable to me for a special purpose. You, Fife—you in particular. But I have already said more than enough. When the time comes, we shall know your worth."

Chapter 4
Flying Colors

After the long tanning process the next morning, Eddie and Raintree were cutting up chunks of cured ham when Eddie decided to share his attempt to negotiate with the captain. Raintree helped himself to one of the chunks and chewed vigorously for a few moments while Eddie stayed quiet, expectant.

Raintree finally swallowed the bite. "I allow," he began, "what you've never heard the story of Captain Barlo. I'ent know all of it meself, but what I can tell ya is that I greatly respect him fer what he done. Listen. Yer familiar with slavin', no?"

Eddie nodded. "I know what it is, but it just doesn't sit with me. I don't know much about it."

"Aye," said Raintree. "It's nothin' I can abide, neither. Well, Captain Barlo is a very proud man, a great man, and it's easy to see why he don't talk about it much. He was studying the law, like his father had before him. All them round scars on his chest are from some sort of ritual for important people that he went through. But you should know he was captured, there in Africa somewhere, I'ent know right where, with a whole lot o' people from his town, his friends, his family, and Mr. Ola too, and they were sold as slaves."

Eddie's eyes widened. "He escaped?"

"Well," Raintree chuckled, "ta sum it all up in a word, that's right, he escaped. But how he did it is a long and most terrible tale, and I only know part o' the story. Sure as I ever heard, everything he tol' me sounded like the very definition of hell itself. He said they were forced onto the slave ship, him and his dear ones, and chained down and stacked on shelves so tight there was barely room to move. Hardly any food. People taking care of their necessities while lying there, without recourse to nothin' dif'rent. Children chained down, too. One of his aunts died right next to him. They came and got her and threw her overboard."

"That is absolutely unconscionable!" shouted Eddie.

"Indeed," Raintree replied, "and not only that, but it just ain't right."

Eddie rubbed his eyes and shook his head. "I can't believe it."

Raintree raised his eyebrows. "Ya mean ya don't believe what I'm tellin' ya?"

"No, no," said Eddie. "I believe you. What I mean is, how can people be so cruel?"

The cook pursed his lips and let out a blast of air. "Well I don't rightly know if there's an answer to that, Fife," said Raintree, "but what I do know, is that many of these slavin' men, these slavers with their slave ships, why… they're our countrymen, fellow Englishmen! Or, I should say, former countrymen. I ain't no Englishman no more."

Eddie closed his eyes, remembering rumors he had heard in the Bristol taverns, talk of immense profits from slavery.

"There were some rough seas," Raintree went on. "The slavin' ship never made port. Cap'n Barlo, and Mr. Ola, they managed to get out their chains, and they helped others out too, and all together the lot of 'em overwhelmed the captain and his crew. But Mr. Ola, when he was struggling to get the shackle off his ankle, he damaged two of his toes so badly he had no choice but to slice 'em off. And then while he was gettin' used to running with his injured foot, he tripped and sliced his leg open. That's the scar he has there. But somehow they managed to survive, and find a safe port for the ship, and well, that was some ten years ago."

"Are we…" Eddie was looking around. "Are we on that slave ship now?"

"No. He traded that ship, and like I said, I'ent know the whole story, but no, this here's a ship what ne'er held a slave, and ne'er will, so long as we skinners have any say in the matter."

Eddie thought about this in relation to what he had hoped to negotiate with the captain. "How do you reckon, though? The captain and first mate escaped from their kidnappers, yet they kidnapped me? The same men who fought to escape bondage, bound someone else to service? I'm talking about myself, but for all I know I'm not the first they've pressganged."

"I see yer point," agreed Raintree, who had moved on to chopping onions. "I've been here longer than anyone 'cept Mr. Ola, so's I can say I'ent seen anybody else pressganged by Barlo. He recruited Jabari and Antonio in Tortuga with signed contracts and all the official whatnot. James Clayton met Antonio a couple years later in the raid on Barbados and asked to sign on with us right away, just like that."

"Did I replace someone on the crew?"

"Nope, we didn't have nobody in that sixth hammock until you came along. Yours is some sort o' special case, Eddie. All's I can figger is that it has to do with the Sea Witch, 'cuz that's who we stopped to see in Cartagena."

Eddie recalled the captain's words about Mr. Ola's determination that he would serve some special purpose, but the mystery behind such a purpose left him ill at ease. It was an enigma poking around in the back of his mind while he performed his shipboard duties.

"I should mention, too, that, uh… I was the one what birthed ya."

"Birthed me?"

"Well, in a manner of speaking. When Barlo dragged ya aboard, knocked out like ya were, he ordered me to remove yer clothes and sling ya in the hammock. So I had to peel ya, just like we did that goat, huh? Right down to the buff, which is why I say it was like birthin' ya onto the ship. And t'was another oddity, 'cuz that is not the regular procedure 'round here to go strippin' others unless they's enemies. But Mr. Ola said ya needed to pass a test. Most o' the time I'ent understand that man. So I'ent ask no questions, I just carried out the orders."

Eddie had indeed wondered about these circumstances and was glad for the information, but still felt like he couldn't quite put his finger on the mystery of why he had even been brought on board in the first place. However, five days of routine had left Eddie feeling at home on the *Capricorn*, and, if he were honest, not missing much at all about his previous crew and ship. He certainly didn't miss his clothes anymore. And if he did happen to think about clothing, which wasn't often at all, he only felt glad to have escaped it. He missed his family back in Bristol in a rather general way, no different than he had before, but he missed Susanna with greater urgency each day, not knowing how long he would have to serve Captain Barlo, nor what was the special purpose he had mentioned. He didn't know what to make of what Raintree had told him—it seemed like no consolation. But he kept his thoughts and questions to himself. He no longer made it his business to consider the ship's location or destination, trusting Captain Barlo's general response about being out in the middle of the sea, and Raintree's claim that they were on the way to Jamaica.

In mid-morning on Eddie's sixth day, James Clayton's call from the crow's nest interrupted the calm. "Ship on the horizon! Starboard bow!"

The crew stopped what they were doing.

"You know what I await, Clayton," shouted the captain.

"Aye, cap'n… and I can spy the colors just now," called the lookout. "She be French!"

"Jabari, hoist the fleur-de-lis," Captain Barlo yelled immediately. "Raintree, get the uniform! All the rest of ye, arm yerselves and get in position! Make haste!"

Eddie began to intuit what was to follow when he saw James Clayton, Antonio, and Jabari take positions in the rigging behind the foresail and mainsail. Above them, already, a white flag with gold fleur-de-lis rippled in the wind. Jabari waved to get Eddie's attention, indicating he should hurry up and join them in the rigging. Eddie climbed up and took his place, and, like Jabari, bit his knife blade firmly between his teeth.

From his position with Jabari behind the mainsail, Eddie saw Captain Barlo standing calmly on deck below them, facing the approaching vessel. What surprised Eddie was that the captain was now dressed in the bright red uniform of a French admiral, with flour dusted over his face. Then Raintree and Mr. Ola took their places, crouched behind barrels placed a couple yards to either side of where the captain stood. Each of them held something long and thin in their hands, something unknown to Eddie, whose purpose he failed to imagine during the long minutes of the ship's approach. He did imagine, however, as he held tight to the ratlines, that someone on the approaching ship was probably scanning the *Capricorn* through a spyglass.

"*Secours!*" Captain Barlo yelled suddenly, startling Eddie. "*Secours, s'il vous plaît!*"

A voice answered from the approaching ship, which Eddie guessed to be only some fifty yards away at that point, and there followed a conversation in French that Eddie could only partially understand. From words like *mutinerie* and *révolte* he intuited that Captain Barlo was spinning a yarn about his crew having abandoned him on the *Capricorn*. He seemed to be drawing the French ship close enough that they could converse without shouting… but suddenly he yelled again.

"Now!"

Everything happened at once: Antonio and James Clayton kicked back and swung out on their ropes from behind their sail, and so did Jabari and Eddie from behind theirs, and Eddie, as he swung over the deck, the wind rushing over every part of his body, saw Raintree and Mr. Ola below him, yanking the threads that ripped Captain Barlo's uniform clean off his body, one half to each side, as the abruptly disrobed captain, his arms and legs outstretched, roared like a lion and threw himself into the clamorous surge, all of them rushing the hapless French sloop, whose strictly dressed sailors gaped in astonishment at the spectacle of the captain's splitting seams even as they struggled to react to the eruption of birthday-suited buccaneers spilling onto their deck.

Not a single shot was fired. Within minutes, the skinners held the French mariners at knifepoint while Mr. Ola and Raintree trained their muskets on the ship's captain.

"*Merde alors*," uttered one of the sailors, who then felt the blade of Antonio's knife press harder against his throat.

"*Les conditions*," began Captain Barlo, "*sont à moi de dicter.*"

From the groans and grimaces that followed, Eddie deduced that his captain told the captured crew to yield all goods and weapons on board, as well as every stitch of clothing they were wearing. Then they would be free to go, it seemed, although Captain Barlo did also invite anyone who so wished to join the skinners.

At this, a young man stepped forward. Ripping off his clothes and throwing them to the deck, he introduced himself. *"Je m'appelle Hamid. Je suis d'Alger, et je veux rejoindre votre équipage."*

"Excellent," replied Captain Barlo. "Do you speak English?"

"I... learning," said Hamid. "Is not easy. Is... very easy."

The skinners chuckled a little, but held firm to their captives, whom they forced, a few at a time, to remove their clothes.

"Je vois que le singe veut nos vêtements..." uttered one of the Frenchmen, who resisted removing his clothes. It was the mouthy sailor that Antonio was guarding.

Barlo exploded into the air, leaping to the sailor and pulling him from Antonio. He gripped the man's shirt and lifted him off the ground some six inches up to eye level. Then, still holding him, the captain turned his face to the sky and roared. No one moved or made a sound.

At the end of the shout, he faced the sailor again, and lowered his voice. "Kick... or spit... and I will hurl you overboard," Barlo told him through bared teeth, "because I am a man. Much more of a man, because I am comfortable in my own flesh!"

The captain held the sailor like this, seemingly without effort, for a long moment. and then said, loud enough for all to hear, "I renounce, I firmly and absolutely renounce, the cloaking of my person with garments created from the labor of my enslaved brothers and sisters, and for which garments the currency exchanged goes into the purses of the slave owners! We skinners, who skin and tan our hides, we trade them in equitable commerce, to the disadvantage of none. And we divide all profit fairly. As the captain, I receive a share no larger than anyone else's."

When Barlo finally set the man down again, he said, "Remove your clothing this instant, or I will rip it from your body."

Eddie had never seen anyone undress so urgently.

After herding the nude Frenchmen into the sloop's galley, where they were guarded by Raintree and Jabari, the skinners set to work gathering the clothes and rendering the cargo: rum, cacao, tobacco, and reams of silk and cotton. Captain Barlo squatted to examine the cotton. He felt the cloth between his fingers, drawing it out between both hands. "This was harvested by my people," he said. "And just look at this cacao! Good as coinage! Harvested by my people! And this rum! Made from the sweat, and the blood, and the toil of my people in the canefields! My people were not invited here, to these lands and seas. Oh no we were not! We were ripped from our homes and our families, only to be sewn up into habits of most noxious provenance! Bind us not! Clothe us not!" Barlo was yelling now, for the French crew, for his own crew, for the world to hear. "That which is wrought from crime and violence, must be healed, or re-purposed. That is our work, the work of the skinners!"

Once Barlo's men had finished moving all the cargo to the *Capricorn*, the captain had the skinners bring the French crew back out on deck.

Barlo detained the new recruit. "Anything else of value on board?"

Hamid nodded, throwing a look of cruel satisfaction to his former captain, who hung his head. The man stood dejected and betrayed in his stripped state, nothing like the proud and comfortable nudity of the skinners.

"*Oui*. There is a… *trésor*," said the Algerian.

Captain Barlo strode over to the vanquished captain and ripped the key hanging on a chain from his exposed neck. He gave the key to Hamid. "Lead me to it," commanded Captain Barlo. "Fife, you come too."

What was discovered beneath a trapdoor under the captain's bed was an oaken chest which, once unlocked with the captain's key, proved to be full of silver bullion. Barlo ordered Eddie to help Hamid carry the chest, which was indeed rather heavy.

Just when the two men were scuffling across the middle of the deck, Hamid in front and with the chest between them, Hamid bent a leg and collapsed. The chest crashed and clanked noisily.

"*Il m'avait poussé!*" yelled Hamid, pointing at Eddie. "He push me!"

Eddie started to protest, but Captain Barlo cut him off. "Clayton. Antonio. Get the trunk to our ship."

James Clayton and Antonio backed away from the French crewmembers they had been guarding at knifepoint. Captain Barlo motioned for Eddie and Hamid to replace them, which meant that Hamid now held some of his former crewmates captive. Once the trunk and all the rest of the confiscated cargo was safely on board the *Capricorn*, Barlo ordered his men to return. Last to leave the French ship were Raintree and Mr. Ola, keeping their muskets pointed at the newly naked enemy crew.

When they all were back aboard the *Capricorn*, and a safe distance away from the vanquished vessel, Captain Barlo ordered all hands on deck.

"We've made a good haul of it, men, and thanks in no small part to Hamid. But Hamid, who has been given a chance with us skinners, alleges poor treatment from one of us already. So tell me, Fife, when the two of you were carrying the chest, did you push him forward?"

Eddie took a deep breath. "I did not push him, sir."

"He did pushed," objected Hamid. "He pushed."

Captain Barlo rocked on his heels, looking back and forth between the two sailors. "So it is one man's word against another."

Antonio stepped forward. "This man lie. Eddie no push him."

The captain walked over to stand in front of the thoroughly tattooed man. "You, who so rarely speak of any matter great or small, why would you make such a grave accusation? How knowst this?"

Antonio pushed out his chest and raised his chin. "Is enough for me to know from Eddie's character. But also I know it from look I saw in this man's eye just before he threw himself down," he added, pointing at the Algerian and squinting his eyes for effect.

Captain Barlo scratched his chin and addressed the newest crewmember. "Is this true, Hamid? What say you?"

"I am a man of my word, a man of faith," he replied. "Why you believe the word of this man? I already see his caress with that other man there like lover. Is this allowed in the eyes of Allah *mon Dieu*?"

The captain's gaze darkened. "For God... I do not speak. I speak only for me. This is *my* ship. These two men are not *like* lovers…. rather, they *are* lovers. And love, you villain, should never be wasted."

Hamid hung his head and muttered a few words in his language.

Jabari's eyebrows raised. "Captain, he saying very bad things about you in Arab tongue that I speak, too. Very bad things."

"Sir," spoke James Clayton, "this rogue quickly betrayed his former captain, and now, just as quickly, he seeks to gain standing with you by betraying whomever he can. Look how he has built up to four of us now insulted."

The captain responded without breaking his stare at Hamid. "Clayton, you and Antonio escort this man to the brig."

In a flash, Hamid hung like a hammock, face down, sustained by the wrists and ankles between his two captors. Eddie and the others listened as the traitor's stream of invective slowly faded away below deck.

"We didn't gain a crewmate," said Raintree. "We gained a captive."

Captain Barlo gave no response to this but spoke to Mr. Ola. "Onward to our rendezvous."

And for most of the next few days, they had the wind against them in rough seas. Eddie relished the freedom of not having to work in soggy clothes, but between his duties on deck and in the galley, he felt exhausted. The rest of the crew was tired, too. The capture of so much bounty from the French ship had buoyed their spirits, but the incident with Hamid left everyone on edge. The men took the captive his food in turns. Whenever it was Eddie's turn, Hamid would shout at him in his language, what Eddie imagined to be curses. Once, with a nasty snarl, he told him in English, "I will take you down." Eddie laughed, but never treated him with the cruelty some of the other men showed him.

On one of these occasions when Eddie was returning from the brig, nearing midnight, he was about to climb back up the second ladder into the moonlight when he overheard a fragment of a conversation taking place on deck just above him.

"...was quick to throw off his clothes and join us, remember? But the Brit was ashamed."

It was the voice of Captain Barlo. Guessing himself to be "the Brit" in question, Eddie ducked back into the shadow, away from the bottom of the ladder, and stayed still.

"From the dead goat's belly, though it was very smelly, the portent was quite clear: we don't want to keep him near," intoned Mr. Ola.

"If Raintree had slaughtered that goat a few days later, would you have been so sure of that portent?"

"The sign and its moment are one. If separate, they come undone."

"When do you reckon we'll reach them?" asked the captain.

"By tomorrow at sunset, 'ere we'll have any fun yet."

Barlo sighed. "I have not made a decision, though I know what my inclination is. But what say you, Raintree?"

"If yer asking me to tell ya which one I'd rather have around, well, there's no doubt, 'cuz there's only one of 'em what's good for anything."

"'Tis true, too, that the one is guileless," added Barlo, "while the other is quite crafty, which, for us, could be an advantage."

"Well it can also be used against us, I reckon," said Raintree.

"Alright men, enough for now. To your posts. The night is odd, eerily still after so much wind."

Eddie's legs began to climb the ladder before his tongue could even begin to move. But the words began to form at the precise moment when the men could hear him before he was visible to them. "I don't know why that Moor keeps going on about inciting a mutiny. Surely he doesn't have any support for it."

When his head cleared the deck floor at the end of the sentence, Eddie saw that they had all stopped their movement and turned to look at him.

"What are you talking about, Fife?"

"Excuse me, captain. I was just wondering about our prisoner. I took him his ration and it seemed to me he was talking about a mutiny. Hard to understand exactly what he means in his English, but I'm fairly sure that's what he said."

The captain and his first mate exchanged a look, after which Mr. Ola began a hasty descent to the brig.

"We happened to overhear you, sailor," said the captain, "but I expect your intention was to report this to me immediately."

"Aye, sir," said Eddie.

"I expect, as well," he continued, "that what you say is true."

Eddie hesitated for just a second. "Aye, sir."

Chapter 5
Fair Trade

Eddie did not sleep well that night. He knew his hastily invented accusation of plotting a mutiny would be denied by Hamid. He knew Captain Barlo seemed to be weighing a decision involving both of them. And he knew, as a diffuse morning light began to slip through the cracks between the strakes, that there was someone, or something, they were on course to encounter that afternoon.

He tried to put his mind into his chores, scrubbing and hoisting and slicing, but he could feel the tense anticipation from his crewmates as well. He was so distracted that he forgot to ask for help applying sunskin, and then when he remembered, he decided that the day was too cloudy to bother. But when Raintree saw him a half hour later, the older man cursed and moved immediately to find a sunskin container.

"Yer shoulders are already as red as yer hair, mate! The worst—the absolute worst—sunburn I ever had, I got on a day like this'un, and it was because I thought the same thing as you, ya fool. Turns out the clouds don't block the sun's rays from burnin' ya to a crisp any more than witchcraft does! Now turn around and let me get yer back and shoulders, then cover the rest o' yerself just like any other day."

The air felt heavier as the day progressed, and a silence grew, as if the clouds muffled all sound aboard the *Capricorn*. Even Jabari was unusually subdued. Whenever there was a break in the cloud cover, the captain and the first mate would look expectantly to the horizon, but to no avail.

Suddenly a deep sound rolled through the fog: a low, ringing resonance of a sort Eddie had never heard. He looked up to the source, and saw James Clayton in the crow's nest, swinging a mallet against a great metal disk. Three times he struck the gong. There was a long pause, and then a reply rang out from beyond the mist: three more peals of similar sound.

The crew stood frozen, silent, awaiting Eddie knew not what. Some of the men had drawn their weapons, but the captain signaled to sheathe them. The only order the captain gave was to drop anchor.

Gradually, Eddie heard a faint splashing sound, growing louder as it approached the *Capricorn*. The captain stepped cautiously to port and peered over the edge. Raintree and Mr. Ola flanked him on either side. Then Eddie and everyone else on board approached, except James Clayton who, from the crow's nest, could easily see into the water.

Eddie saw nothing at first, only gently rolling waves, until there crested, slightly above the surface, the glittering silvery tail of a large fish… which flipped over and was followed immediately by the head of a woman, her long blond hair trailing in the water. As she bobbed in the waves washing past her, it became clear that she wore nothing over her shoulders, back, or chest.

Jabari, staring intently, moaned with such great anguish that it seemed he would jump overboard at any moment.

Quite suddenly, Eddie believed in mermaids.

"Hail, ambassador," spoke the captain.

"Captain Balthazar Barlovento," said the mermaid. "We have awaited your return. Have you procured your barter?"

"Aye, sister, of all the qualities demanded."

The mermaid appeared to be floating effortlessly upright as she spoke. "There were no demands, captain, only the agreement of a price for what you seek."

"So be it. We spoke of certain qualities, as I recall: youth, vigor, and a good disposition."

"Indeed. And an attractive appearance."

"On this latter quality I will let you pronounce judgment."

"Well, where is he?

"He is here. On board."

The mermaid scanned the men's faces. "Is he one of these scurvy mutts peering down at me? Is he that large fellow there, keening like a randy hound?"

"No. Not any of the men you see."

"He lies," shouted a new voice. Eddie looked to see that another mermaid had arrived, bobbing a short distance back from the other. The second mermaid had a slightly darker complexion than the first, and long dark hair.

The captain smiled at the new arrival, then gave his order "Jabari! Fife! Bring the captive!"

After replying with their 'Aye, captain,' Eddie and the Egyptian descended to the brig. Eddie, still wary, felt a small sense of relief. It seemed to him that whatever decision the captain had made, had fallen to his favor. He also felt relieved to be partnered with Jabari, who was as tall as the captain and probably the strongest man on board. Between them they subdued the agitated Algerian and dragged him up to the deck.

"Here he is," shouted Barlo over Hamid's curses.

"Let us see him," replied the first mermaid.

The captain motioned for the men to keep Hamid away from the rail. "First, supply me with the location I seek."

The scornful laughter of the mermaids carried easily over the water. They both turned and began to swim away.

"Wait! Dear... sovereign beauties! No need to be so rash!" In his uncharacteristic desperation, Captain Barlo leaned so far over the scuppers that Mr. Ola and Raintree each grabbed one of his shoulders to hold him fast.

"Be steady, be staid, lest yourself become the trade."

Shaken, the captain looked at Mr. Ola and nodded.

"Well?" came the voice of the first mermaid. "You would make us wait still longer?"

The captain motioned for Hamid to be brought to the deck rail. Hamid's eyes widened upon seeing the mermaids, but then he shrugged his shoulders. "Water woman. Is about this?"

"Turn him around," insisted the second mermaid.

Jabari and Eddie spun Hamid around slowly in a complete circle. The mermaids looked at each other and submerged, while the captain and crew of the *Capricorn* were left to wait tensely for them to reappear.

Hamid broke the silence. "You want I go with pretty water woman? I go."

"Remember what we discussed," the captain murmured to Hamid, holding up his hand while rubbing his thumb and first finger together.

As the late afternoon sun began to break through the clouds, the mermaids surfaced. "We do not accept your trade," spoke the first mermaid. "Leave immediately or suffer the consequences."

The captain gaped and swung his head, his arms outstretched. "Most righteous sirens… I have fulfilled your conditions!"

From both mermaids there arose a whooping shout, and instantly there appeared, from a hill on the islet behind them, a piercing beam of light. The radiance threw such intense and focused heat against the mainsail that its fabric began to smolder in a dark, smoky patch that expanded quickly.

The captain's gaze followed his outstretched finger up into the sails. "Look there, Clayton! Piss to it!"

And as James Clayton desperately and ineffectively aimed a stream of urine at the burning patch below him, the captain continued shouting orders to his crew with the intent of pulling the *Capricorn* into retreat. The mermaids watched the spectacle, laughing again, while the beam of light moved to hit the middle of the foresail.

In the confusion, Jabari unhanded the captive and ran off to weigh anchor. Quick as spite, Hamid grabbed Eddie and called out to the mermaids, "You no want me alone! You take two? One, two!"

Busy at the helm, the captain could neither abet nor abort Hamid's offer, but the mermaids were quick to shout encouragement.

"No! Let go!" yelled Eddie, kicking the other man's shins. But Hamid would not loosen his grip. He began to spin Eddie around in a circle, each man pulling on the forearms of the other. At a moment when Eddie's back was to the rail, Hamid released his hands from Eddie's wrists. It was just enough slack for Hamid to push his advantage, and Eddie toppled backward over the rail, headfirst into the ocean. The last that he saw before smacking rough and hard into the waves was Hamid against the sky, jumping out beyond him.

***

Eddie regained consciousness lying on a beach. He rolled over and spat seawater from his mouth, then lay on his back, heaving. When he opened his eyes and squinted into the sun, he looked up into an array of legs and arms and faces and breasts and long hair. Three nude women towered overhead, scrutinizing his recovery.

His body reacted naturally. One of the women pointed this out, saying, "He's fine. And… we won't need the rope."

The women began to walk away. Eddie hoisted himself onto his elbows and saw a hill rising above the beach not far beyond them. The memory of the light beaming from the hill came to him, and he realized that after Hamid had pushed him off the *Capricorn*, he must have arrived somehow to the mermaids' shore. There was no one else on the beach, and Captain Barlo's ship was nowhere in sight.

The women were heading toward the hill. They all had long hair—two of them dark in color and the other blonde. The one with the darkest skin carried the rope. The tallest and the blonde each carried, hanging limply over their arms, something like the glittering silvery tails of large fish.

Quite suddenly, Eddie no longer believed in mermaids.

As Eddie watched them, the blonde one turned back to him for a moment, motioning for him to follow them. He stood up uneasily. When he began to walk, he realized in the act that his locket and his knife were still on his person, but something felt strange. Blood began to drip down his face due to his upright position and energetic movement. Feeling for the source of the wound, he discovered a large gash along his forehead. It seemed much longer than it was deep. Eddie held his hand to it and continued along behind the trio of women.

They scaled the hill quickly, curving around on a path that led them to disappear inside a burrow that had been built into the slope of the hill just below the crest. The entrance to this shelter opened inland, such that no part of the dwelling could be seen from the ocean. Arriving a few minutes later, Eddie found that there was no door, only a thinly woven curtain. He pulled it to the side and stepped across the threshold.

"Out!" yelled the darkest-skinned woman, who sat on a low stool. She had already donned a multicolored robe that covered most of her body. "Out! Who saying you entering?"

Eddie jumped back beyond the entrance. While he stood for a moment trying to peer through the curtain, he heard the women murmuring inside.

"Excuse me," he said, a tad urgently. "I've got a large gash on my head, and I wonder if maybe you have something to help?"

"Help," called the same woman with a snort. "You not even knowing how much we already helping, you stupid man not knowing how to swimming. Now, you can opening curtain."

Eddie drew back the curtain and stepped through. The three women stared at him. What little Eddie could see of the robed woman's flesh was accentuated by many piercings, with metals of various hues gleaming from her ears, nose, and eyebrows.

"Now you here starting learning some things," she said.

"Thank you for rescuing me," Eddie said.

"I no having interest rescuing you," continued the woman, "but my sisters, they pitying you, and they pulling you to shore. The other man—he the real barter… well, he disappearing. So it is you to doing."

"Doing… what?" Eddie asked the robed woman, who was obviously in charge, although he would have preferred to ask the question of the other two women, who were apparently more charitable, and definitely still naked. He had become accustomed to nudity among the male sailors aboard the *Capricorn*, but he was not at all used to so much female nudity, nor to being naked himself around women.

"First thing you doing. You calling me Empress. That one there Queen," she said, pointing at the tallest of them, "and that one Princess." The Princess was the blonde, and although bronzed from the sun, she was still the lightest-skinned. She was also probably the youngest, Eddie thought, estimating her to be slightly older than he.

"Princess," continued the robed Empress, "I charging you care of this man who not knowing much of nothing. You teaching him how to swimming, fishing, hunting, in the time he waiting for someone to coming getting him. You accepting charge?"

The Princess, who was rinsing a cloth with water from a large basin, gave Eddie a very serious look that wiped down his body from head to feet. "Yes. I will do my best, Empress."

"Very good. Then, loss of other man, man who swimming correct, not hurting our trade."

The Princess wrung out the wet cloth and took it to Eddie, who sat on the ground so that she could bind his forehead with it. The cloth smelled of a pungent herb. She told him to lie down on a thin reed mat that she unrolled for him, and to keep the cloth on for a while. With that, the three women left him lying on the ground of their shelter, with no indication of where they were going, what they were doing, or how long they might be gone.

Eddie lay still but could not resist looking around their shelter. There was a central fire pit, with a roof opening above it and a stack of firewood with a couple roasting spits to one side, and hanging nearby were a few pots, spoons, and knives. There were three hammocks strung beyond the fire pit, along the back edge of the cave-like dwelling, where an overturned canoe rested as well. Nearer to the entrance, some spears and nets were propped against the wall. There were a number of baskets, one of which seemed to be emitting light toward the ceiling. When he sat up, Eddie saw that a mirror was resting on the basket lid.

He laid back down and took stock of his circumstances. He was not sailing. He was not aboard the *Summit of Virtue* nor the *Capricorn*, and he didn't know when he might next board a ship, or which, if any. And he was naked, in the island home of three nude women who seemed to live as sisters with no one else around. At least, he thought, they did not appear overly hostile, and at least by now he was used to being naked. From his conscription to Captain Barlo, he had learned first-hand not only just how much of life can be lived without clothes, but also how sensible and pleasurable it is to do so. From what he knew of the three women, he would say they seemed to agree.

Eddie allowed himself a small smile and closed his eyes to rest.

When he awoke sometime later, his dream image of Susanna's face dissolved into the face of the Princess, who was unwrapping the bandage from his forehead. He studied her face: blue eyes, thin lips, and a small nose. The freckles on her cheeks extended down to her chest. Eddie noticed, too, that the angle of the light through the roof opening had shifted considerably during the time he was asleep.

"What... how long did I sleep?"

The Princess regarded him with clinical detachment. "The things men want to know about themselves..."

Eddie exhaled heavily as she unpeeled the last of the bandage from his skin.

"There," she said. "The gash on your head is looking better. It will close soon."

"I thank you."

"I've been out most of the day, and I've returned with dinner. Can you sit up? Do you think you can get a fire started?"

Eddie propped himself up. "Yes."

Just as Eddie noticed some sort of animal stretched along the ground near the curtain, the Princess picked up the dead iguana by its tail, grabbed a spit, and deftly reamed it from mouth to tail. Leaning the shafted lizard against the wall, she told Eddie she'd be back soon with some wild squash.

Eddie got up slowly, a little light-headed. He found some tinder and kindling from the firewood pile, and some dried palm fronds. Picking up the mirror, he held it into the sunlight from the roof opening, angling it to reflect and concentrate the rays into the fuel. Before long, the flames were high. He added several small logs from the pile. When the Princess returned with handfuls of small gourds, Eddie had just placed the spit on its rack over the flames.

"Nicely done," she said. "Perhaps you're not as useless as the Empress thinks."

Eddie smirked. "This mirror damaged the sails on the *Capricorn* very efficiently."

"Your captain was forced into a hasty retreat," said the Princess with a laugh. "Wasn't he expecting a bit of a fight from us?"

"I don't know. But he thinks you're mermaids. We all did."

The Princess skewered the gourds onto another spit and added it to the rack. "If you knew how to swim, you'd appreciate how difficult it is to give the appearance of a mermaid. With that false tail binding your legs, you end up using the belly more, and the arse, too."

Eddie considered this a moment. "You know, I saw Captain Barlo strike awe into another ship's crew by having a uniform ripped from his body. It was all very clever, with loosely sewn stitches and hidden wires. Why wouldn't he consider the possibility that he himself was being similarly fooled by you?"

The Princess sighed and turned the spits. "Each man sees what he wants to see. Some of these idiot sailors catch a glimpse of the animals that the locals call manatees, and then they go write in their logs the most pretentious nonsense: 'I saw a mermaid this morning off the starboard bow! By the by, not nearly as beautiful as the ancients would have us believe.'"

Eddie laughed. "People can be very stubborn. We also hear what we want to hear. Maybe I am mistaken, but to me you sound Welsh."

The Princess smiled. "You have a good ear. I am from Pembroke. And you?"

"Bristol," said Eddie.

"Ah, but I don't think much on Wales anymore."

"What is your name?"

Eddie's question brought a grimace to her face, and a slight hesitation. "Princess."

"Is that your given…"

"Of course not. But I can't tell you my real name because I don't want you to slip up and use it. You'd get us both in trouble."

"Why's that?"

The Princess fanned the flames and turned the spits again. "We have a nice arrangement here, the three of us 'mermaids.' But the Empress is very strict, and that's because she wants to protect us. As you can see, we live very unconventional lives. And you, I've just met. I can't trust you with facts that could be used against us."

"I see," said Eddie. "Unconventional, indeed. I frankly never imagined there'd be so many folk living naked out in the world."

"Growing up where you and I did, people don't imagine life like this. But here in the tropics, as they say, the light slants differently."

From the Princess's uniformly bronzed skin, Eddie guessed that she must have been living for quite a while in the tropics. "Can you at least tell me how you ended up here?"

"Shipwreck," she said. "Use that knife you've got there to scrape some scales off the iguana."

Eddie unsheathed his knife and began scraping, thinking he would probe for more details later. But the silence grew prolonged, and he asked, "Where did the Empress and the Queen go?"

"Where do you think? They went to find your crewmate, that man who jumped off the ship."

Chapter 6
Swimming Lessons

The iguana tasted like something that wasn't quite rabbit, and wasn't quite fish, Eddie thought, but rather somewhere in between: not unpleasant, although certainly unfamiliar. The wild squashes, on the other hand, had a flavor and texture unlike anything he'd ever tried. He found them very difficult to swallow.

He and the Princess ate alone, and when they finished, she rinsed out his bandage and reapplied it. He learned that one of her duties was to collect rainwater and parcel it out into several kinds of containers for different purposes. The basin that the Princess was using for his bandage had a curative herb that she had crushed and stirred into the water.

It wasn't until after dark that the other two women returned. They had searched thoroughly all around the islet without finding any trace of Hamid.

"I'm exhaust," said Queen. "Br… Princess, you take first wash. Diss man… wassa your name?"

"Eddie."

"Eddie sleep in your net, Princess, and you sleep in mine. Tu… Empress net is big enough for her and for me."

Eddie had been wondering where he would be able to rest. Now he wondered whose hammock was whose.

"As you see, we take watches through the night," the Princess told him. "Starting tomorrow night, you'll be expected to take your turn."

She pulled a sword out from underneath a pile of blankets. Eddie's eyes grew wide as he watched her wield it first in one hand, then the other, her moves modeling grace and power.

The Queen and the Empress were watching him. "Don't getting ideas," said the Empress, shaking her head and waving her index finger. "So many man knowing nothing. But that other man, he knowing escaping. Better barter."

"Go sleep," the Queen told Eddie as soon as the Princess had stepped out into the night.

"Which…" Eddie began to ask.

"Dat one," said the Queen, pointing at the Princess's hammock.

Eddie pushed down on the hammock to test its strength, noticing that the ends were tied around thick roots that ran down the walls of the shelter. It would hold him easily.

He climbed in, and then saw that the Queen was hanging the last corner of a blanket that separated the Empress's hammock from the rest of the open space.

"Good night," he said.

There was no answer. He was soon asleep.

***

Over a breakfast of coconut and some tea sneakily borrowed from the Queen's supply, the Princess asked Eddie if he knew about sunskin. He told her he had been using it on the *Capricorn* and asked her if she knew how to make it. She didn't know all the ingredients; she only knew they had to trade for it: shells, fish, iguana. As he rubbed on a generous amount, helping her with her back in the same way she helped him, he began to understand the role of sunskin as a commodity among these naked Caribbeans.

The full day was devoted to Eddie's lessons, beginning with the easiest: iguana hunting. On the beach, the Princess rolled some wet sand into a cylinder of the approximate size of an iguana's body. She had Eddie practice harpooning the false lizard from increasing distances, telling him that if he learned the spear quickly, she'd teach him bow and arrow some other day.

When they moved to the large rock where the iguanas liked to sun, she tied a long rope to the end of the harpoon. "You have to get down low and move very slowly to approach them," she said. "Slowly!"

Eddie crouched and crawled, feeling awkward about his uncovered hindquarters sticking up in the air, but managing to get quite close to the rock. He turned back to see the Princess nod. He raised the spear, slowly, and launched it successfully into the side of his victim.

"The rope!" Princess yelled, and Eddie grabbed the end of it just as the iguana slid from the rock straight into the ocean. Eddie dug his heels into the sand and pulled, surprised by the strength of the swimming iguana. The harpoon's hooks stuck tight inside the animal. The Princess joined him, and that made the difference: they were finally able to drag to shore the iguana which, by that time, had lost a lot of blood and could only feebly resist.

Eddie pulled his knife from his sheath and slit the lizard's throat.

"Not bad," said the Princess. "This is a big one. We'll all eat well."

Eddie noticed her trying, and failing, to hide a smile.

They took the meat back to the shelter, where the Queen had already prepared a fire and was set to begin cooking. The Princess decided there was time for a quick swimming lesson before eating, so she removed Eddie's last bandage and led him back down to the beach. From the iguanas sunning on the rock, they went a bit further east, to an area where there was a shoal ideally suited for swimming lessons. The Princess plunged in.

"Get yourself in here, Eddie! Look, I can touch bottom and the water's up to my chin. For you, it'll be up to your chest."

"How large is this shallow area?"

"Goes out quite a ways. There's a reef out there somewhere that forms a natural wall. Don't be scared."

Eddie bristled. "I'm not scared."

"Then hurry up, get in here and get your whole body wet. The salt water will finish healing your forehead."

Eddie waded in and squatted to wet his head. Since the water was so shallow, it felt warm and soothing.

"There. See? Like a large bathtub, it is. Now, first thing we do, is practice breathing."

The Princess led him through a series of exercises, submerging to exhale and then surfacing to inhale again. As she was prompting him to move more quickly, and to start to move his arms as well, he gulped some sea water and stopped to cough it out.

"There are plenty of ways to swim with your head out of water," she told him, "but you need to be able to swim underwater, too."

"Why?"

"Diving, hiding, comfort when swimming long distances. Stop resisting."

They kept at it a while longer before returning to the burrow to eat a much more sumptuous presentation of iguana meat—this time it had been boiled in a stew with coconut and various vegetables, including a particular kind of seaweed. When the Princess mentioned to her companions that Eddie was making progress, the Empress merely harrumphed. The Queen was more enthusiastic but urged them to rest before hurrying back for more swimming.

When they finally did make it back to the shoal some hours later, the Princess was able to teach the breaststroke to Eddie in such a way that he mastered it after an hour or so.

"This is a wonder," said Eddie. "I feel like a mermaid myself. A merman, I mean."

"You're doing well, but you still have much to learn."

"Where did you learn to swim?"

"Here in the ocean, on my own. Nobody swims or bathes in Wales."

"Right. Nobody swims in Bristol, either, and any man what does swim has to wear linen breeches."

The Princess laughed. "Imagine that!"

Struck by her response, Eddie chuckled too. "It's really quite difficult to imagine, now, isn't it?"

"Such an impediment!" exclaimed the Princess. "Why swim with something that could drag you down to drown? Although, come to think of it, I suppose it's rather like swimming with that mermaid tail. It makes for a very different kind of movement altogether. Much less natural."

Before they left the water, the Princess had Eddie lean backward while she supported his shoulders and thighs until he got used to floating on his back.

"Be still," she told him. "You can believe that the water buoys a massive ship, but not your small frame? Imagine you're a little fishing skiff."

Eddie kept trying to adjust his body. "But a boat is built with a precise shape for floating," he said.

"Ah, but people have been around longer than boats, don't you think? And our bodies float naturally. Hold still!"

Eddie finally stopped fidgeting. Face to the sun, he felt relaxed, but also exposed. As he floated, he asked, "Do you ever miss clothes?"

The Princess thought for a moment. "Clothing can be very fancy. Sometimes it can be very warm, a source of comfort. But no, especially here in the tropics I don't miss clothes. Least of all the strictures that women are expected to wear. Corsets, and petticoats, and horrible shoes... you can only imagine. Oh no, not one bit do I miss clothing!"

Still on his back, Eddie kicked his legs to keep them afloat.

"Why?" she said. "Do you miss them?"

"I think, for me, it's not that I miss wearing them. It's that, especially now, staying with you three women, I do sort of miss the privacy."

"Oh—because you're the only man. I understand. But don't you think our privacy might be important to us as well, as women?"

"Yes. Which is why I think you must be so accustomed to the lack of it at this point that it no longer crosses your mind."

She laughed. "That's right. Until you came along and started talking about it!" She let go of Eddie to cover her chest while making a face. Eddie stood, covering his groin and grimacing back at her. Soon they were splashing each other and laughing, not at their bodies but at the very concept of covering them.

On the walk back, the Princess continued the conversation. "You know, you're not the only man that any of us women have seen. You don't need to be so self-conscious. And besides... well, the Empress and the Queen love each other. I don't think they are interested in men's bodies at all."

"Ah! I see," said Eddie. "And you?"

It was the first time Eddie saw her blush. "I'd say that I am just as interested in men as I am in women," she answered.

"Well! You don't hear that every day, do you? I don't think I've met anyone like that before."

"I bet you have. I bet we all have. People are just afraid, or ashamed, to talk about it."

Eddie mulled this over for a few moments as they continued walking. He noticed the Princess staring at his chest.

"Will you tell me about your locket?" she asked.

"Oh! It's a gift. From a young woman I know in Bristol."

"Someone special?"

"She is special to me," Eddie sighed. "Her name is Susanna Hemsworth. I'm beginning to wonder if I'll ever see her again."

"Do you miss her?"

Eddie surprised himself by having to consider his answer over their next few strides. "I miss her as I knew her," he finally said. "But just as I have become someone she might not even recognize, she, too, may have changed considerably by now."

"Do you think maybe," the Princess began, adding a delicate pause, "she found someone else?"

Eddie stared at the woman next to him—strong, smart, graceful, beautiful, and nude. "These things happen, right?"

They continued on in silence. Eddie stopped to pick up a promising piece of driftwood, indicating vaguely to the Princess that he would see what he could carve from it. In fact, he had already imagined what he would make with it, as a gift for her.

When they arrived at the shelter, the Empress and the Queen were not there, a fact that, according to the Princess, meant that neither she nor Eddie would need to take a turn on watch that night.

"Today," said the Princess, "you've practiced hunting and swimming. Tomorrow we'll work on bow and arrow. But it seems to me that I should assess your skills in another area, too."

Eddie shrugged his shoulders. "What area is that?"

"Kissing," she said.

Several hours later, falling asleep next to the Princess in her hammock, Eddie gave up on even trying to count the number of new skills he had learned with her.

***

Over the next several days, Eddie dedicated time when he was alone to carving his driftwood gift, but he spent almost all his time with the Princess. It was natural that they reached a deep level of intimacy, sharing many moments of charged tension: her chest pressed into his back and her hand on his as she helped him steady the bow and aim the arrow; their mutual delight in seeing each other's appendages buoyed by the water as Eddie learned to dive ever deeper. In their frequent conversations, he helped her recall more about her life back in Pembroke, and she did ask him about his family and his life in Bristol, but she seemed more interested in the days he had spent aboard the *Capricorn*.

One late afternoon, after a meal of crabmeat—Eddie had just learned how to catch crabs with a net that morning—and the creamy, delicious fruit the locals called wanabans or guanabanas, the Princess began another round of questioning. "That day we saved you, I counted eight men on board the *Capricorn*. Was that the whole crew?"

"As far as I know," Eddie said. "It was a small crew."

"And I saw three cannon openings on the port side, so I assume he has six total. Do you know how much shot he has?"

"There was quite a bit in the stockroom…"

The Princess wrinkled her brow. "How much?"

Eddie paused. He shifted to a colder tone of voice. "Why do you want to know so much about Barlo and the *Capricorn*?"

She stood up quickly from the stone where she had been sitting. "Are you still loyal to him, then? Is that it? Don't you care about me?"

Eddie stood too. "Among the many things I've learned here, I've learned I care about you very deeply. But, as you'll no doubt recall, I don't even know your name."

The Princess huffed and crossed her arms.

"There is still much that is unclear to me," Eddie continued. "What is this about someone coming to pull me away from here, from you? What is this about Hamid, who seems to have escaped some sort of barter?"

"I've told you before. We have a very precarious, protected situation here…"

"Yes," Eddie cut her off. "You have indeed told me that before. You want more detail about me? Then give me more detail about you. You can start with the shipwreck."

The Princess grew quiet, took a few steps away from Eddie, and stood still, looking out to sea. Then she began walking toward the beach. Eddie caught up to her.

"You listen to me, Eddie Fife," she was saying. "I don't have much. I don't really own anything at all. But something I do own is my own story. I can choose whether, and how, I might want to tell it to you, or to anyone. Only because I've gotten to know you as someone honest, someone to trust, will I tell you my story. But because I don't feel I trust you completely, at least not yet, I will give you only the appearance of my story, keeping many of the details known only to me."

"Thank you. I…"

"Don't interrupt! Just listen. And whatever you do, keep this to yourself!" She sighed. "My name is Bronwen. I grew up in Pembroke, like I told you. I have a large family… had. I had a large family. When I look back on them now, I wonder if anyone really misses me, when I was just one more sister, one more cousin, one more daughter. It seems like my whole childhood was one big rabble of children running around, and our parents and the other grown-ups trying to get us to eat, or to learn our sums, or to sleep… or rather not paying any mind to us at all."

"Sounds familiar."

Bronwen stopped walking and glared at Eddie. He understood she was reminding him not to interrupt.

"So I would often take my clothes off. Whether I was indoors or outdoors. It just felt good. It felt right. And sometimes I wasn't alone. A sibling or cousin would join me. And one day my Aunt Addien, of all people—such a wretched person—of course it was she who found me outside running around naked with my cousin Gavin. We were eleven or maybe twelve years old at that time. She screamed and yelled and made such a fuss, even though all we were doing was picking wildflowers and collecting beetles. Can you guess what happened?"

"Uhmmm," said Eddie, uncertain as to whether she really wanted him to answer.

"I was sent to a convent, that's what happened. Two days after the incident with Aunt Addien, my family sent me away, never to see me again. The nuns, first thing they do, they shear off all my hair. I used to have hair all the way down past my bottom! It's taken me years to grow it back, and it's still not as long as it used to be. At the convent, I had to sleep on a hard floor with a thin blanket. All day long I had to wear a heavy, scratchy habit. A convent, as you probably know, is supposed to be a holy place. The nuns get married to God, and all that. Well, the convent where I was,

was not a holy place. It was one of the wickedest places I ever saw. You get too many rules, you end up with a lot of depravity.

"So I had to escape. For months I pilfered old sheets and shifts until I had enough to fashion a rope. Huh. It wasn't lost on me that all that cloth was going to lead the way to my naked freedom. When I finally did wiggle through my cell window one night, the escape was easier than I thought.

"I ran through the dark, following my plan to make it to the docks before daylight. I filched some food, slipped by a drunken guard and hid on board a merchant ship. By the time they found me, we were almost to the Caribbean. And then, well, one of the sailors tried to have his way with me, but I kicked him hard between his legs. So he tied me up and hit me, and then forced me. And I cried so hard but I would not let... I would not let that man break me.

"And fortunately, a short time later, the ship hit a reef. Most of the men on that ship drowned. Some got away on a lifeboat. I don't know what happened to the one who forced me, and I don't make it my business to care. But I say it was fortunate because I immediately ripped off my dress and—frankly because I had to, because I wanted to survive—I taught myself to swim away from that disaster. I sucked down a lot of seawater, but I was not going to let myself drown when I felt such freedom.

"It took me months, Eddie—and remember, I'm not giving you all the details—months to find this island. The Empress and the Queen were already here, and they accepted me quickly when they saw I already knew how to swim, fish, hunt and cook. I've been here past three years now.

"The only good thing about that convent was that it was where I started learning English. Otherwise, how could I tell you my story? I've shared it with you, including even my real name, because I trust you. You need to trust me.

Trust me that if I'm asking questions about the *Capricorn*, it is a matter of safety and survival for us mermaids."

Eddie looked down at the sand, or out into the surf, anywhere except into her eyes.

"Eddie. You can talk now."

"I, uh… I don't know what to say."

Bronwen sat down on the sand. "What do you think about my story?"

"You're very brave. And I'm so sorry about your family… and the awful sailor… I'm sorry for all that happened to you."

She took his hand and pulled him down to sit next to her. "Yes, all of that happened to me. But, Eddie, the most important part is what I did about what happened." She sighed. "I've learned that what defines us are the choices we make about our circumstances."

They held hands and watched the setting sun paint the horizon. Then, as the sky darkened and the stars overwhelmed, Eddie shared the many details of his story of conscription and service under Captain Balthazar Barlovento. When he had finished, Bronwen embraced him, and pulled him to her, and as he rolled with her in the surf on the sand, he came to understand the salty sexes of woman and man in their natural element, arrayed like just another pair of sea creatures, or a mollusk searching for its shell.

Sometime later, Bronwen remembered they needed to return to the shelter because it was Eddie's turn for watch. They walked, hand in hand, back to the lookout spot over the roof of the burrow. They spoke further, in hushed tones, not without observing the horizon, the wind over the waves, the night noises, and the general state of their surroundings.

Past midnight, in a lull of silence, Eddie renewed conversation to stay awake. "What is it that Captain Barlo wanted from you mermaids?"

Bronwen looked over each shoulder before responding. "It's a recipe. You have to let the crabmeat soak with the guanabanas for a couple hours."

At Eddie's confused look, she motioned for him to follow her away from the shelter.

"We were too close to the roof opening," Bronwen explained. "My sisters might have been listening."

"Understood."

"Barlo wants to know where the Sea Witch lives."

Eddie stroked his scruffy chin. "Why doesn't he just ask her? They obviously know each other. I saw them have a conversation," said Eddie.

"I don't know. They seem to have a mysterious, complicated history."

"So..." Eddie continued, "uh, why didn't you tell him? Wasn't I the price for that information?"

"Whether it was you or that other sailor didn't matter. We never had any intention of telling him where she lives."

"Do you in fact know?"

"Oh yes. Quite precisely."

"You're saying it was a false bargain, an arrangement designed to fail," Eddie said. Then he opened his eyes wide and raised his eyebrows. "The Empress. She sat right here on this hill, with the mirror, ready to damage the sails, while the Queen swam with you to the *Capricorn*... so, why does she keep talking about how Hamid would have been a better barter? For what?"

"Why do you think I've been teaching you to swim and hunt?"

"So I can pull my weight around here. Help you all with your life."

"We don't need your help." Bronwen swallowed hard. "You're our barter for the Sea Witch."

Chapter 7
The Art of Escape

In the early hours before dawn, when the Queen came for her turn on watch, she found Eddie and Bronwen sitting far apart from each other in silence. Bronwen got up and went to her hammock, but Eddie went to lie down in the Queen's.

By the time the sun rose, Eddie could tell that Bronwen deeply regretted having given him so much information. He had become surly and standoffish. When she finally pulled him by his arms to get him to move, as he was swallowing the last bites of a small breakfast, she led him down toward the beach with a net over her shoulder and a basket over her arm. Once they were away from the burrow, she squeezed his hands and looked him in the eyes.

"Eddie. What I told you is the truth. That doesn't mean you have to like it. It certainly doesn't mean I agree with it."

He broke eye contact but replied. "You rescuing me was just a way to catch me. And I fell for the bait."

"You would rather have drowned? Is that what you're saying?"

"You could have rescued me and then released me."

"You wouldn't have survived, would you?"

"I'm a resourceful fellow. And I have a knife."

"Eddie, I didn't know much about what was happening. The Empress is the one who planned it all out. How was I to know who Barlo was going to throw overboard? And it turns out there were two of you, but you're the one who needed rescuing."

Eddie smirked. "That lucky bastard Hamid has no idea what he missed."

Bronwen frowned. "I also did not know that I would end up caring about you, loving you."

"Yes, and that makes two of us."

Bronwen put her arm around Eddie's waist. "Forgive me."

Eddie turned to her and kissed her forehead. "There's nothing to forgive. You're right—you rescued me. But next time I won't need rescuing."

Bronwen smiled. "Yes. At least now you can swim. This morning we're going to work on fishing… which should give us plenty of time to hatch a plan."

Eddie had fished a few times, years earlier with his older brothers, using a rod on the banks of the Avon. With Bronwen, he learned a method with a weighted net, a bit different from netting crabs, that required two people to maneuver. The silvery blue fish that frequented that particular shoal were small but numerous, and quite tasty, according to Bronwen.

"The coloring on these fish looks familiar," said Eddie.

"Yes, we use the scales from these fish to make those mermaid tails. It's a very laborious process!"

They fished until they had two full nets' worth of catches in the basket, and then they climbed from the beach up onto a large rock jutting out toward the ocean to sit for a spell.

"I think you may have told me last night," said Eddie, "but I wasn't listening by that point. What exactly is the Empress wanting to trade me for?"

"Nobody makes sunskin like the Sea Witch," said Bronwen, "and she keeps the procedure top secret. In trade for you, the Empress could receive enough of it, for the three of us mermaids, to last all the rest of our lives."

Eddie nodded.

"However, being the Empress, that's not good enough for her. She wants to trade you for her usual amount of sunskin plus some of the Sea Witch's own special sunskin. It's made with gold dust. The Sea Witch has kept it exclusively for herself, but she's allowed the Empress to think that maybe she will trade some for the 'right man.'"

"That would be me," Eddie guessed, with a strange mixture of pride and resignation.

"Perhaps. Remember, the Empress wanted the other man, Hamid. She thinks he would be the better choice for getting what she wants."

"And that's why she ordered you to teach me how to swim and hunt and fish."

"Yes."

"I can escape. But would you…"

"Eddie!"

Before he could react, Eddie felt something whish past his left hip. Instantly he felt an arm around his throat as he was pulled into a standing position, the blade of his own knife pressing under his chin. Then he heard a familiar voice.

"Give me fish basket, woman, or I cut throat."

Eddie brought his hands up to pull against his attacker's arms. "Ha… mid…" he groaned.

Bronwen's face paled, but she recovered quickly, noticing how the stranger's prominent ribs confirmed his desperation. She stood and picked up the basket.

Hamid cocked his head toward the beach behind them. "Drop on sand."

Bronwen saw it was only about a six-foot drop: it was where Hamid must have hidden when he had sneaked up on them. Despite Eddie's attempts to tell her not to comply, she extended her arm and carefully let go of the basket, which plopped down without spilling any fish.

Hamid loosened his grip around Eddie's neck, and as he removed his arm, he grabbed Eddie's locket and yanked hard. The chain popped.

Eddie spun around to face the Algerian, but Hamid had already leapt down to the sand. He threw Eddie's knife and locket into the basket as he grabbed it and ran off down the beach yelling, "I will find gold dust!"

Eddie jumped from the rock and raced after him.

"Stop, Eddie!" Bronwen called. "He's armed and he's desperate!"

Knowing she was right, Eddie slowed his effort and let his pummeling legs come to a halt. He rested his hands on his knees and took a few deep breaths as he watched Hamid turn from the beach, far ahead of him, and disappear into the brush.

Ruing the day that Barlo had attacked that French ship, Eddie turned around and saw Bronwen approaching him.

"How's your neck?" She kissed the red marks where the knife blade had been, and where the chain had broken.

Eddie stared at her wide-eyed. "He stole my knife! And my locket!"

"At least you're not hurt," she said. "And at least he didn't steal the net. We can fill it one more time and take the fish back to the burrow like that, in the net."

Eddie just nodded. "Did you get a good look at him?"

"Yes. He's obviously starving. He's probably gorging himself on raw fish right now."

"Using my knife to scale them! He is a most villainous traitor, that man."

As they repositioned the net and waited for more fish, Eddie narrated for Bronwen, not for the first time, the several instances up to that point of Hamid's treachery, ending with renewed emphasis on the stolen knife.

Bronwen began to pull in the net. "There are other knives back at the burrow, remember?"

"I don't think you understand. That is a very special knife to me. I know its heft and thrust with my eyes closed." He didn't mention it, but he was thankful that he had already finished carving his gift for her.

"I'm sorry, Eddie." Bronwen sighed. "But at least it was a knife you lost, and not an eye, or a pint of blood. Now please help me pull in our only catch."

***

When they arrived at the burrow with their paltry pile of fish, and the Empress and Queen heard about Hamid's attack, the Empress was quick to reinforce her position.

"You seeing? This other man, Hamid, he being very clever, very daring. Now he holding fish, basket, knife, necklace and he wanting finding gold dust. Better barter."

"Donch you tink, *cara imperatrice*," said the Queen, "dat such a… clever man, were he our barter, would not tink twice to take advantage of Sea Witch? Den where would you be?"

"Bah," replied the Empress, fussing with her robe. "The Sea Witch being my friend? No. I caring about her? No. If problems with barter, not mattering anything to me."

"But *la Strega del Mare*, diss witch, she is an enemy with power," said the Queen. "And, not anymore would be able we trade wit her."

"Not needing trading anymore after this barter," came the reply. "You, Princess, you finishing teaching hunting fishing swimming this man?"

"Yes, Empress. He has learned these skills well and has acted bravely."

"You wanting staying with him?"

The question caught Bronwen off guard. "I…"

"I'm prepared," interrupted Eddie. "I'm prepared to be your barter..."

"Not even knowing…" muttered the Empress.

"...on one condition!" Eddie finished, improvising as he spoke. "I…

"No asking condition!" the Empress shouted. "No your place!"

"I… I am in no place to ask for conditions," Eddie admitted. "But Br… Princess can."

The Empress arched a ring-studded eyebrow. "Getting knowing yourselves very well, Bronwen?"

Bronwen stood. "I care about Eddie, yes. I told him my name, but not yours or the Queen's. Why wouldn't I tell him who I am? He grew up not far from where I did, and we know the same language well. And he has earned my trust."

"How?" asked the Queen.

"He could have tried to take advantage of me on numerous occasions these last few days. But he did no such thing. On the contrary, he has treated me with respect. He has shown trust to me, and I to him."

"So. Like I saying," said the Empress, "you wanting staying with him?"

"Maybe," Bronwen replied. "Here's what I propose. When you trade him to the Sea Witch, trade me too."

"Hmmm…" thought the Empress. "Could trading even more sunskin. Maybe trading for jewelry too."

Eddie turned to face the woman who had taught him so much over the past week. "But why would you do that?"

Bronwen looked him straight in the eyes. "I think I'm falling in love with you. I think maybe you love me too. I want us to have more time together, to know for sure."

Eddie felt speechless in the face of her calm and logical assessment. After a few moments of gazing into her face, he managed to say, "We go together, then."

"I am agreeing," said the Empress, who pointed to the shelter entrance. "And this being just in time."

The sound and the sight were simultaneous: just as Eddie and the mermaids saw the splash of bright red, blue and gold fly across the threshold, they heard the bird's raucous squawk.

"She arriving," said the Empress.

Bronwen reached for the fruit basket and held out some berries for the boisterous macaw. "It's the Sea Witch's messenger," she explained to Eddie. "We need to get to the beach."

Eddie's three hostesses jumped into action, and he watched, fascinated by their preparations. The Empress dug through a barrel until she found a crown to don. The Queen, similarly, rooted through a box from which she withdrew a tiara and an elaborate necklace to wear. Bronwen, however, gathered all her various weapons and possessions to take with her, according to her plan of leaving this home of hers for good.

From behind a rock outside the burrow, Eddie fetched the gift he had fashioned from the piece of driftwood. He held it out to Bronwen: a beautifully carved mermaid in profile, her right arm raised, her hand in her flowing hair. She was about the length of Eddie's arm. Her fishtail curled behind her as she gazed off to the right. "This is for you, Bronwen."

The departing Princess's eyes grew wide in surprise. "Eddie, it's lovely! Such precious craft!" The Queen looked on approvingly. Even the Empress seemed impressed.

Bronwen exhaled sharply. "When you started making this, you thought you would be leaving alone. I did too. But

I'm going with you, Eddie… so I'm going to leave this here, with my sovereign Queen and Empress, as a sign that we'll come back someday."

She handed the mermaid to the Queen, who delighted in its details for a moment before placing it in her own hammock for the time being.

They walked to the beach in a solemn procession behind the Empress, her gaudy robe billowing in the breeze. Eddie, so naked that he did not even have his knife or his locket to wear, helped Bronwen carry her possessions. The macaw flew ahead and landed on a low shrub near the shore. But there was nothing on the horizon.

"We waiting here," announced the Empress.

One by one they began to sit down in the shade of a palm, resigned to a long wait in an uncomfortable silence. Even the macaw had grown quiet in the afternoon heat.

"And so Eddie says to us goodbye," spoke the Queen, interrupting the general stupor. "But before you leave, man, I decide I telling you *la mia storia*."

This was met with a harrumph from the Empress. "Why wasting breath? Never seeing this man again."

"Dat is exactly why I tell him, Tuluná," retorted the Queen, "and dat is exactly why you should speak, too. Diss Eddie, he know we are not *sirene*. Our fish tails, all that is fake. Better he know why we do what we do."

"But he can giving names! He can telling others who we are!"

"Bah. *La Strega del Mare*, she already know. I want diss Eddie to know what we women tolerate. He already learn from Bronwen, her *storia*. Now he learn mine."

Eddie looked out to sea. There was still no ship on the horizon—plenty of time for a story or two.

"I want you to know, Eddie," began the Queen, "dat I no like man very much. I no like no man very much at all.

Probably including you. But at least so far I can tolerate you. And Bronwen, she like you and trust you. More than we," she added, pointing to herself and the Empress. "I tell you why I no like no man very much at all.

"I am from Genova. I grew up in a very large *famiglia…*"

"Me too!"

The Queen stared at Eddie. "I no expecting you to talk. Only listen. Yes?"

Eddie smiled and shrugged.

"Many mouts to feed, my *mamma* had. My *papà*, he no do nothing, only drink. No help at all wit seven *bambini*. So we were very poor."

The Queen spat into the sand, startling Eddie, who noticed she had done so with a ferocity that had not altered her excellent posture. She took a moment to adjust her tiara and necklace before turning to look at him.

"What would you do, eh? I was middle child. No favorite, no oldest, no youngest, no spoiled. I turn twelve years of age, and my papà suddenly he like to touch me. Somebody, I tink it was da neighbor, start to talk about da convent, just like what Bronwen already told you dat happened for her. But I ran away from home before I got near any cursed convent."

At this invocation of the cloister, the Queen crossed herself in a vigorous reflex. Eddie chuckled a little at her guileless irony.

"And what choice did I have? If no convent, I have choice of get married, or go to *bordello*. At least at da bordello I get to live wit other women, and only have to see men for making money. So, dat was my choice. I chose bordello. It was an easy choice for me.

"I loved the other *prostitute*, all of dem. Almost all of dem. I no love any man who came to feel me, who came to smile false smiles and embrace false and kiss false. Deese men, dey look at my breasts or my legs like I was another piece of *carne* at the butcher's shop. But no my heart. My love, it was wit other women.

"Dere was one man who like me too much. He was sick in da head. He tie me up and stole me away from da bordello. Next ting I know, I am on a boat. A really big boat going who know where. But I act, I am an actress, I act like I am *tranquilla, contenta*. I lie to diss man, I tell him I so happy he rescue me from da bordello. Because he is just a man, he believe me. Sorry Eddie but is true, is why I tell you no be such idiot as most men.

"Anyway I acted and acted like I so *felice* wit him, for weeks, for months, while he protect me from da other sailors, but he hit me all the time, he abuse me. He give me diss scar, see?" She pointed to a long mark along her right thigh. "He slash me witta knife one night when I told him I was too tired for him.

"Finally I had an opportunity. He was drunk and he break a bottle and I grabbed it. It was like a round knife, dat bottle, and I stab him right in da heart, diss man who stole me and abuse me. I stabbed… and I twisted dat broken bottle, Eddie. And so of course da other sailors catched me and beated me. But da captain, he order dem let me be. Da captain was very *cattolico*, very superstitious, and what happened was dat it was eighteen of August, day of Santa Elena. And dat, Eddie, is my name: Elena. So da captain should have kill me, because da man I stab, he die. But he no kill me because it was day of my saint. So he put me on a lifeboat, and dey abandon me at sea."

Eddie noticed that the Empress was dabbing a few tears from her eyes.

"Dere she is," said Elena, pointing to the Empress, who had stood and walked away from them toward the shore. The Empress stooped down and began to dig in the wet sand as

Elena continued. "She is one who save me. I no understand how I was still living after six days, because I had just a little bread and water with me in lifeboat. But Tuluná, she found me and brought me here, and here, Eddie, is where I am most at home. No man. No clotes. Sun and rain and good food. Eddie, you will not take diss from us. Only memory of us you can take."

"Thank you for sharing your memory with me, Elena," said Eddie with a respectful nod.

"Look now, Tuluná she want tell you her *storia* too."

The three of them walked to where Tuluná had been sculpting in the sand. When they arrived, Tuluná and Elena embraced and kissed, an act Eddie had not seen before.

Bronwen spoke to Eddie. "See what she is building, like a little well? This is her way of telling her story."

Tuluná sniffled and wiped more tears. Finally she said, "You telling story Elena."

"*Naturalmente, cuore mio,*" whispered Elena. "You Eddie, you have to see dat diss hole full of water, it has a name for da people of Tuluná, the people who are called Maya. Dey call diss well a *cenote*. Is dat right?"

"*Tz'onot,*" said Tuluná. "I calling it *tz'onot.*"

"Except the *cenote* is no on da beach," continued Elena. "It is near da beach. Very large. Very deep and too steep to climb out. Many cenotes dere are where she lived."

Tuluná had upended little sticks and shells and other bits of debris around the well in the sand, and pointing at them, she said "People." Eddie could see that the well, to scale, was meant to be very deep.

"Tuluná was a princess of her people. Dey had a… *credenza*? Like a faith, dey had, to sacrifice young women like Tuluná to cenote. Why?'

"Bringing rain," said Tuluná. "Like you saying before, superstitious."

"So da people dey gather, and den dey trow in a sacrifice, even dough da Spanish, dey making da Maya change gods. Da time came when da sacrifice was Tuluná. But she had a plan to no drown. To swim. She knew how to swim in ocean, and she practice no breathing for a long time, for several minutes."

Tuluná interrupted her partner to draw attention to a tunnel she was excavating with her finger, connecting the bottom of the well directly to the sea.

"*Si, amore mio*, I will speak it," Elena told her. Then she clarified for Eddie. "Tuluná knew dat many *cenotes* had tunnels dat lead out to sea. So on da day her people trow her over the edge, she took deep breat, and *per fortuna*, da water in the cenotes is very clear. She quickly swim out of view, and she see two tunnels she start to test for passage. No da first one, but da second one led out a long way, with spaces for her to be able to lift her head and take breat. And after a couple hours like diss, because da tunnel would split and she would have to go each way to see which way worked, and sometimes she could not even see and could only use her hands to feel and her nose to follow da smell of salt whenever she could breathe, she finally made it to ocean."

Eddie watched Tuluná reenact her escape by throwing a small shell into the well. The ebbing tide pulled it through the tunnel, and she caught it in her hand when it came out into the edge of the surf. Then she looked at Eddie. "You seeing now why is good knowing swimming?"

Eddie nodded.

"Tuluná was very angry at her people," Elena continued. "She no want return. She hided, she survived, until she could steal a boat, and den she set out to sea. After many *prove e tribolazioni*… many adventures dat I no speak right now, she came to diss island where dere was no anyone. She fought away many who came here after her, but me she welcomed, and Bronwen… and what are we going to do now without Bronwen?"

Elena had begun to cry, and the macaw to squawk. The loud bird took flight toward the horizon just as Eddie saw the outline of a ship appear. As he sat, surrounded by three women for whom he now held a deep reverence as astoundingly brave survivors of trauma and architects of their fate, hugging each other and trying their best not to shed so many tears, he felt a great uncertainty, yet also an immense gratitude just to be alive. It wasn't hard, he found, to remind himself that there were many worse fates than being together with the one he knew he was beginning to love, naked and healthy under the sun. He had contemplated running away from them all, but Hamid had shown how unfavorably that path would turn out. On the contrary, he knew he would go through with it, Bronwen at his side, to be the barter for these women. Had the Sea Witch already enchanted him to her beck and call?

As the ship of the Sea Witch drew closer—and Eddie could see it was slightly larger than the *Capricorn*—the Empress Tuluná composed her face into a look of steely resolve. Queen Elena, drawing courage from her partner, copied her expression while adjusting both the Empress's crown and her own tiara. Princess Bronwen and Eddie, as they cleared the brush from the small boat hidden near the shore, prepared to row out to meet their fate.

Chapter 8
Something for Nothing

Elena needed to go with them, so that she could row back with the precious sunskin. As the three of them approached the ship, Eddie spotted its flag, a cream-colored banner with two identical dark brown rings side to side in the center. It was difficult, at first, for Eddie to recognize the Sea Witch, who, far from dancing as she had done when he first saw her, was standing still and firm, as if she were part of the ship, like a figurehead of ebony. She wore nothing except some gold jewelry that flashed sunlight from her ears and navel. Her gaze bore into him as their rowboat approached, and the first thing she said surprised him. She placed her hands on the rail, leaned forward, and called out, "Where is your heart?"

Eddie looked up to her in confusion. "I… I don't… It's right here," Eddie finally said, pointing near his left nipple.

The Sea Witch laughed suddenly, and kept laughing as if it were the funniest misunderstanding imaginable.

Eddie smiled. Bronwen smiled.

Then the Sea Witch turned, just as suddenly, quite serious. "Not your inside heart. I mean the one you were wearing on the outside."

"It was stolen."

"Who stole it?"

"A traitor. Hamid by name."

The Sea Witch scowled at Eddie for a long moment. Still scowling, she addressed Bronwen. "This is very serious, mermaid… but less so than your theft of this man's inside heart."

"Yes," said Bronwen. "Love is a serious matter. And if I have stolen his, then… he has also stolen mine."

"I see," replied the Sea Witch, smiling brightly. "Nonetheless, you and your sister will still receive your trade. Higgins, bring the smaller trunk!"

And just as Eddie began to understand who might have been summoned, there appeared on deck his former first mate from the *Summit of Virtue*, as nude as everyone else.

"Mr. Higgins!"

"Fife," came the nonchalant reply. "Fancy meeting you here."

Higgins lifted a wooden trunk that must have contained the barter and opened the lid so that all could see what was up for exchange.

"What do you think of this trade, heart-stealer?" asked the Sea Witch.

"I'm… part of the trade," Bronwen replied.

The Sea Witch raised her eyebrows and crossed her arms over her ample bosom. "What is this? What says the Empress? This is not the trade that we agreed on."

Elena spoke up. "Diss idea is no from the Empress. But the Empress is agree… for a larger trade."

"Please accept that I can be of service to you," said Bronwen.

The Sea Witch began to pace back and forth along the deck, thinking through possible benefits and drawbacks of this modification to the agreement. Eddie heard an intermittent clattering, like the noise of wooden blocks tossed together, coming from somewhere on her ship.

"I have many skills," Bronwen called out. "I'm the one who taught him to hunt, fish, and swim as requested."

The Sea Witch stood still and looked down at Bronwen again. "Is it pride that makes you speak so, or is it love?"

"Both," she replied.

"Then look upon my crew here," said the Sea Witch, motioning all of them to the rails. There congregated a group of eight women and men, all nude each alike, of a full range of skin colors, and they were joined by her macaw, who perched on the foremast, and a cat-like animal that climbed onto the rail. It had a long snout and a ringed tail the likes of which Eddie had never seen.

"These are very skilled people," continued the Sea Witch, "and animals. Your skills… I hope that you have used your skills to train Fife well, but your pride I don't need. And as for love, accept my gratitude for confirming that Fife is capable of it."

"But…"

"Hold your tongue, Fife!" shouted the Sea Witch. "Mermaids of legend, I still offer you your trade, but I will not give it to you until this man passes inspection. He must come aboard first, for examination by my physic, and if he passes, I will give you your barter. You must trust me."

"And if he no pass?" asked Elena.

The Sea Witch put her hands on her hips. "Then there is no deal. Is he not of good health? You remember I specified this condition precisely."

Eddie turned to Bronwen, who stood stoically, a single tear sliding down her cheek. "I will come for you, Eddie," she whispered. "Do not doubt that. Go in love."

"I love you," Eddie whispered back.

"Come, Fife!" ordered the Sea Witch. He kissed Bronwen quickly on her cheek before climbing the rope held out to him by Higgins and one of the other crewmen.

Once Eddie was on board, Higgins gripped his shoulders and moved him backwards a few paces to a crate, where he pushed him into a sitting position, and then stared him in the eyes for a moment. "This'll be a little odd, mate, but just let it be. We've all been through it."

As Higgins backed away, so did everyone else, except one woman who strode right up to Eddie. She appeared to be a native Caribbean, with some graying strands in her long, straight, jet-black hair. Eddie guessed she must have been at least fifty years old, perhaps sixty.

Saying nothing, she reached out to squeeze Eddie's shoulders and upper arms. Then she peered into his eyes, nose, and mouth, and tugged on his beard, which had grown rather full. Stepping to his sides, she looked into his ears, and parted his hair to look at his scalp. She placed her head on Eddie's chest to listen to his heart, and then she sniffed under his arms.

"Stand," she told him, and when he did, he realized that her height did not even reach his shoulders. Before he knew what was happening, she was smacking his abdomen repeatedly. Just as suddenly, she manipulated his penis and scrotum for a few moments, and sniffed his groin.

"Turn and bend," she said. Eddie felt very strange, but as he turned, he noticed that no one was paying any attention to any of this, except the Sea Witch, who stood a few paces away, and Bronwen, who could not see much of what was happening from her position down in the rowboat. When he placed his hands on the crate and bent over, the woman slapped and pinched his buttocks, and separated them to inspect his anus. She squeezed both his thighs, and calves, and then she lifted his left leg and started poking at the sole of his foot. She seemed to be watching for his reactions when she poked different areas. Eddie was amazed at how long this took compared to the rest of the process, and then marveled again at the entire long routine repeated with the sole of his right foot.

Finally she released his right leg. "Stand," she told him again. "Sing."

Eddie wrinkled his brow. "You want me to sing?"

"She needs to test your voice," said the Sea Witch.

The woman sang a pitch, moved up to another pitch, and then gestured for him to repeat. Eddie sang the pitches back to her. Then she sang a series of three pitches, then four, and five. Each time, Eddie was able to repeat the sequence accurately.

"Well?" asked the Sea Witch.

"Well," nodded the woman. "Very well."

The Sea Witch stepped to the rail and raised her voice. "Mermaid sisters, you have honored our trade arrangement of something—this man—for nothing, or rather the ability to wear nothing under the sun when using sunskin. Fife, lower the trunk for them. It is your barter."

The trunk had already been noosed. Eddie hesitated.

"Ha! You are wondering what will happen if you do not comply," said the Sea Witch. "Let me tell you. If you do not comply, I will not return you to the mermaids. I will force you to wear clothes—women's clothes—until such time as I decide to drop you in the middle of the ocean. Understood?"

She motioned, and a few of her strongest-looking crew members approached. The thought of having to don clothes again—women's or not—and especially when no one else on board had to suffer them, gave Eddie serious pause.

Remembering what Bronwen had whispered to him, he made up his mind. He lowered the chest over the side of the ship, and Bronwen caught it, placed it on the floor of the rowboat, and undid the noose. Mechanically, she bent over to open the lid, revealing many small clay containers.

Elena began to rummage through them. "A fews of da pots are red," she said. "What is?"

"Those contain my special variety of sparkling gold," said the Sea Witch. "My gift to the Empress for keeping her word."

"It is of your own confection?" asked Bronwen.

The Sea Witch stood in steely silence, arms akimbo, for a few long moments. "Do you really think I would pass off someone else's inferior product as my own? You insult me. Now go before I change my mind."

The Sea Witch turned to her crew. "Raise anchor! Higgins, to the helm!"

Bronwen and Elena began to row away. The Sea Witch spied on Eddie as he watched Bronwen disappear. After a few moments, she interrupted his reverie. "Come, Fife. We shall have a palaver."

As he followed her aft, a noise grew louder—it was the same sound of jostling wood that he had heard earlier. They turned toward the port side of the captain's quarters, and Eddie saw what was making the sound: several rows of halved coconuts suspended by yarn or rope from various eaves and boards, clicking and clacking and colliding as they walked by. Eddie saw them to be planters, each coconut bowl with its own herb sprouting from within. They proceeded to the stern. The cat-like creature scampered along near them, but two crew members moved away so that he and the Sea Witch were left alone.

"Higgins says," she began, "that you are a sharp man. Good with words and good with a knife. Is this so?"

"Yes. Yes… ma'am."

"I'm pleased to know it. Here is a new word for you to learn. Repeat with me: Oshuna."

"O shoo nah," pronounced Eddie.

"Good. That is my name, and it is how you refer to me."

"Yes, ma'am."

"Next word: *Ogba*."

"Ohg bah," repeated Eddie. "What's that?"

"That's the name of my ship."

Eddie looked around, from bow to stern, as if to question whether she meant the ship they were on.

"You are surprised that I am the captain, Mr. Fife? Why so?"

Eddie found no ready answer.

Oshuna paced back and forth in front of him, studying him from head to foot. "That part of you, there, at the crotch of your legs," she began, "that hangs down like a chili pepper with a pair of guavas behind… well, it is very like these papayas that sprout from my chest."

"Ehr…" stammered Eddie. "But one hangs from a man, and the others from a woman. And their purposes are quite different. What has that to do with…"

"And these melons that top your legs," she said, circling behind Eddie, "are they not the same as mine?"

Eddie thought a moment before replying. "Yours are much bigger. And darker."

Oshuna came around to stand eye-to-eye with Eddie, and stared at him with a raised eyebrow, unmoving, for a long moment.

"What I am telling you, Englishman, is that these appendages of yours are no more a part of your skeleton than are these appendages of mine. No matter which fruits bloom from our blessed bodies, underneath we are all the same trunk: only a skeleton."

As Eddie did not respond, she continued pacing, gesturing with emphatic grace at the appropriate anatomical references. "Our fruits are sweet, and succulent, don't we know it! And they bring forth and nourish new life! But 'tis little difference what fruits one brings to a captaincy. What matters is what's on the inside of the skeleton: the brains… and heart… and gut."

"Then you are a captain witch? A witch captain?"

"I am indeed the captain," replied Oshuna. "But I am no more a witch than you are an idiot."

She smiled while Eddie squinted, struggling to process her response.

"Look. There are other ways to live. You've seen this already. Do you let someone else tell you what you should like to eat, or what you should like to sing? Should I let others tell me whether I am a witch or whether I can be a captain? I never let anyone tell me, in all my years, that I cannot reveal my body to the waves and to the wind, to the sand and out to the stars. And it does not matter to me if I am alone or among others when I do it. And you—you and everyone else—should have the same freedom. Though you come to me bare already, you are free to wear clothes if you like. I would not order you to be stripped like Barlovento did. But I hope you find that you share our preference."

"Yes, ma'am."

"Whatever skills you learned and honed with Barlo… and with the mermaids… use them here as well."

She clapped her hands, and the odd animal with reddish-brown fur, ringed tail, and a long nose that had been sniffing around nearby, came to her immediately. A moment later, the macaw perched on her raised arm.

"What is the word for this animal… captain?" asked Eddie, expecting to learn another exotic term.

"Oscar."

"Oscar?"

"That's his name. And this is Onesimus," she said, pointing to her macaw.

"I mean, what is that kind of animal called?"

"You've never seen one before? Some people call it a cusumbo, some call it a coati. I found him when he was an orphaned cub, and now he is a part of the crew."

Eddie watched as the animal rolled at Oshuna's feet. "Does he help keep pests off the ship?"

"Yes indeed," came the reply. "He's useful. You'll see. Oscar, go find Higgins…"

The coati jumped up and began to scurry toward the prow.

"Follow him, Fife," Oshuna said with a nod after the animal. "Let Higgins show you your duties."

And so Eddie hastened to follow Oscar, making his way back through the clutter of hanging coconuts as gently and as quickly as possible. By the time he caught up, Higgins was waiting for him with the coati on his shoulder.

To Eddie's surprise, Higgins made to embrace him. Oscar jumped down and ran off.

"What a twist our lives have taken, Fife!"

"Yes, sir," said Eddie. "Yes, indeed!"

"Well, now… and part of that twist is you don't have to call me sir. We're just crewmates now."

As the older man led the younger around the ship, they swapped stories covering the events since that foggy night on the pier at Cartagena. Higgins showed great interest in Eddie's experiences with Barlo and then with the mermaids.

"I still don't know how they divvied us up between Oshuna and Barlo," said Higgins. "Maybe they flipped a coin. But what I can say is that your lot was the more adventurous one. In my case, why, I didn't wake up naked not knowing where I was. Nothing like that. Oshuna just took me by the hand, and it was like I didn't want to struggle. She's definitely some sort of enchantress. She led me on board, and I saw that not only she but everybody was naked, and she told me to take my clothes off when I felt ready. I could barely believe it, but I felt ready in just a few minutes.

"And do you know, Eddie… it's the damnedest thing. Thanks to you sneezing like you did—which, you know, maybe you could have tried to stifle that or something—well anyway thanks to that, I don't know when I'll get back to Bristol. I miss my family!"

Eddie started to apologize but Higgins kept talking.

"And yet I love it here. I love sailing so much more than I did before. And I love Oshuna, you should know. I have, well… a new life with her."

"What do you mean?"

"Maybe it's too soon to know, but here on board the *Ogba*, we're lovers. She tells me about the place we're headed—she calls it the community—and it sounds wonderful."

Higgins turned his gaze toward Eddie's chest, where his locket used to be.

"I told her about you because she asked. I told her about Susanna, how she's from a very well-off family. Everybody in Bristol knows the Hemsworths to be good, charitable people. Really quite a bit above your station, if you don't mind me saying. You must have tickled Susanna's fancy somehow. And I'd wager she's never even seen you in the altogether like I'm looking at you right now! But you're healthy, and strapping, and smart. Young love, and all that. You know… it's not too late, maybe you could convince Oshuna to let you get back home."

"I did try to convince Barlo, without success. And I do miss Susanna. But I love Bronwen, you know, the mermaid. And Bristol… the Hemsworths… that's all a world away now, isn't it?"

Higgins and Eddie looked to the deck, where all around them, their clothes-free crewmates were going about their chores. Higgins nodded. "A world away."

Eddie spent the rest of the evening learning from his former first mate not just the daily routine, which, after all, was similar to what he already knew, but also the broader objectives of their captain. Higgins led Eddie to understand that the sunskin was running out, which was putting Oshuna on edge. To make more, he told Eddie, she needed a few ingredients, including a special one that only one person could obtain. That person, Karaya, was the woman who had inspected him when he came on board.

"What's the special ingredient?"

"I wish I could tell you, mate, but I don't even know myself. I don't think it's a plant—she grows all those here. There were a few implements she needed that she obtained in Cartagena. All I've heard is something about a cove on an island where Karaya's people used to live. But that's not where we're going. She told me as soon as we have you on board, we're going to the community."

"Wait just a moment… So she had this rendezvous set up with the mermaids… but how did she know the mermaids would bring me, and not someone else?"

"I don't know, mate. It was exactly what she expected, as if she foresaw it happening."

"She's a witch."

Higgins laughed. "Surely. But she's also a terrific captain and a wonderful woman. Oh, and she did say there might be another stop—something about a rough bed."

A sound interrupted them: the low rumble of someone blowing through a conch shell. Higgins explained it was time for dinner. The entire crew began to gather on the main deck, where they held hands in a circle and intoned a short phrase of thanksgiving that Eddie would come to learn, since it was recited before every meal: *Ounje yii wa lati inu ogba wa ati lati ogbon wa. A dupe fun o.* Higgins whispered to him what he had learned from Oshuna: it was Yoruba for "This food comes from our garden and from our skill. We are grateful for it."

A more delicious shipboard meal Eddie had never eaten. The fish was delicate and flavorful, not tough, and the vegetables had been roasted and seasoned to perfection. He learned that in addition to the hanging half-coconut planters he had seen earlier near the captain's quarters, there was a modest garden plot, perched on a shelf accessible from the back of the poop deck, whence came the yams and squash, and a viscous green capsule he learned to call okra. All of this was accompanied by casabe bread, whose nutty flavor put him off at first, although he soon favored it over the hardtack he'd been wrestling down his throat before. Its flavor was further enhanced by the wondrous smile on the face of the young woman who brought him his plate.

Chapter 9
Cut Loose

On his first morning aboard the *Ogba*, Eddie already felt at home. After the all-male crew on the *Capricorn*, and the all-female time spent with the mermaids, he found it refreshing to be among mixed company. He noticed that he and Higgins seemed to be the only people on board who hailed from England, or even the north of Europe. Most of the crew had African, or Asian, or Mediterranean, or Indigenous features. Of course, no one wore clothes. Eddie, being the kind of person to ponder such things, wondered if, just a few weeks earlier aboard the *Summit of Virtue*, he would have felt as much at ease among so many people of different backgrounds, had everyone been cloaked in the garments of their own cultures and religions.

Eddie had assumed he would be working with Higgins, whom Oshuna had made her navigator. But that was not the case, nor were Eddie's skills needed in the busy *Ogba* galley. Instead, Oshuna ordered him to apprentice with Waniyo, who was something of a repairman. Trained as a cooper before he escaped slavery, Waniyo had made all the many rain barrels on board and sealed them with a method that Karaya had shown him using the sap of the rubber tree. He had a few prize tools that he carried with him in a large pouch, and Eddie followed him around to learn everything from patching sails to replacing worn-out planks.

Higgins introduced Eddie to everyone on board, and it was a challenge for Eddie to remember all the names. But there was one person whose name he had placed a priority on learning, repeating the syllables again and again, their sound as strange and fascinating to him as she seemed to be herself: Yewande. He guessed her to be about his own age, and she was also approximately his height. Her skin was as dark and smooth and shiny as ebony. When Higgins had introduced her, she had not spoken, but merely smiled, and the contrast of her strong white teeth with her dark face completely disarmed Eddie, just as it had when she had given him his food the night before. After two days aboard the *Ogba*, he had not heard her utter a word, neither to him nor to anyone else.

Yet this, too, interested Eddie greatly—the mix of languages he detected all around him. English was common enough on board, but he didn't know how many other tongues were being spoken, or had been learned, or by whom. Since he had not yet heard Yewande speak, he did not know if he would even be able to communicate with her. Yet as he watched her weaving gingerly among the herbs growing from the hanging half-coconuts, testing a leaf between her lips or monitoring the soil with her fingertip, or tending the larger garden off the poop deck, where she stepped through the gourds as delicately as a gazelle in spite of her precarious position on a platform jutting out over the rough toss of the surf, he felt her to be something of a kindred spirit, because he observed that she kept to herself, and that she focused on her work without being standoffish or antisocial.

On the morning of Eddie's third day aboard the *Ogba*, after a breakfast of casabe bread and fresh fruits, Oshuna addressed him casually.

"Are you feeling at home here now?

"Yes, captain."

"Does your heart have a new home here?"

After a moment of silence, Eddie replied. "It may be so."

Oshuna swung her head to look him in the eyes. "Do you know Yewande watches you as much as you watch her?"

Eddie fought the blush but knew he could not control it. "No, captain, I did not."

To his surprise, the captain looked gravely disappointed. "That mermaid, hadn't she trained you in love? Either she was a poor teacher, or you are a stubborn student not to notice such behavior in the very one you are noticing."

Confused by being forced to think about Bronwen and Yewande at the same time and in such a circumstance, Eddie could only conclude that it must have been true: he was a stubborn student.

Oshuna waited a bit for his response. None came. She sighed and changed the topic. "I trust that you've at least mastered an easier skill for which I require your service today: swimming. We're approaching an oyster bed I frequent. You and Yewande will be working together."

Eddie smiled at this, which, in turn, brought a smile to Oshuna, who said, "Now I see that you are not so stubborn, but merely that you are still unskilled. Pay attention to your surroundings, Fife. Be gentle with your fingers on the rough bed. And be gentle with hearts—yours, hers, and everybody else's."

"Yes, ma'am."

***

Eddie assessed that the sort of deep diving that had been such a delight to learn with Bronwen would not be necessary that day, because the oyster bed extended from slightly above the surface to not that far below. Waniyo tied the *Ogba*'s rowboat to an iron ring that he had driven into the bed some years earlier and set to work scraping off the loose oysters lying in the sun.

Yewande, without any hesitation, submerged herself and began pulling on the underwater oysters to see which ones she might be able to remove by force. Eddie took a deep breath and followed her, and as soon as he was completely submerged, he saw Yewande pointing to oysters that she had tried to remove using only her hands but that had not come loose. He set to work on those with the knife that Waniyo had lent him. As the two of them moved along the reef, his rate was much slower than hers, and he saw that he was needing to breach for air more often than she did; however, it was often the very large oysters that were more firmly attached, for which the knife and his strength were needed. Eddie and Yewande would place the oysters in the net bags that floated from their shoulders, and swim back to the boat to dump them out whenever they were full.

After about half an hour, at a moment when they were both underwater, Yewande tapped his shoulder and motioned for him to follow her. She swam a little further down and around, carefully holding on to the reef to keep herself submerged. Eddie followed and saw that she was pointing at a very large specimen, the largest they had seen that day. He nodded, approached, and began to slice off some of the surrounding shells just to be able to get an angle on the huge oyster.

They both needed to surface for air several times. At one point after Eddie had taken a deep breath, he submerged again just in time to see Yewande facing a large, quickly moving, bright green moray eel, its long dorsal fin undulating in the light, its huge jaws sprung wide open. Eddie raised the knife in an instant, but Yewande stayed his hand. She pulled a fish from her net bag and held it out for the eel, and then let go of it just as the eel's open mouth snapped. Eddie's surprise grew as he saw the eel allow Yewande to run her hands along its sides, arching like a friendly cat, even as it was swallowing the fish. She produced another fish and went through the routine again—

this time the eel swam through her legs, rubbing against them—but then she needed to surface for air. The eel took a moment to look at Eddie, who stared back at it, still wary, and then it simply turned around and swam back where it had come from, somewhere around the edge of the reef.

Amazed, Eddie surfaced again just as Yewande was on her way back down. When he joined her again, he sawed away some more around the massive oyster and finally had space to slide the blade under the surface of the prize. He wondered why Yewande stayed with him, assuming she just wanted to see him free such a large oyster. After all, she had been the one to find it. Or, he thought, perhaps the eel would return, or some other animal familiar to her. But after he had given a few slices, she swam to him. She covered his left hand, which was gripping the shell, with hers, and began to twist the oyster against the force of the knife. Eddie winked at her to signal that he understood the tip. But she kept her hand where it was, even grabbing onto his right shoulder with her right hand for greater stability, and kept twisting until the oyster was finally cut loose.

When they both surfaced for air, one hand each on the oversized oyster, she told him, "Sometimes it takes two to free a stubborn third." It was the first time she had spoken to him, and everything about that moment etched itself deep into Eddie's memory—the timbre of her voice, the fading feeling of her hand where it had gripped his shoulder, the sunlight on her skin and hair, the droplets falling from their faces as they treaded water for a moment before swimming back to the boat, the smile that grew on her lips as he simply watched her without responding.

Once they were back on the boat with Waniyo, Eddie peppered Yewande with questions about the eel, and she told him that since she had befriended it some years earlier, she always brought some fish for it.

"A knife is not the solution for everything, you see? We were visitors to the home of the eel."

Eddie felt a little ashamed. But Yewande smiled at him again and added, "I do appreciate that your instinct was to protect me."

Soon Eddie realized that not only had he made the wrong assumption about the eel, but that he had also been incorrect to assume that they would return immediately to the *Ogba*, which lay at anchor further out beyond the bed. Waniyo was rowing them away from the ship and closer to shore, making a curious kind of bird call from time to time as he did so. Yewande motioned for Eddie to stay quiet. For some while they continued along in this fashion, following the shore in and around a couple of inlets, never moving far out-of-sight of the *Ogba*.

They rounded into an estuary, and that was when a response to Waniyo's call was heard. He began rowing toward the shore. As soon as the boat hit the soggy edge of the river, a woman appeared from behind some shrubs. She was as dark as Waniyo and Yewande, and she wore a brightly colored but faded shawl with a simple burlap skirt. Waniyo motioned her aboard, and Eddie moved closer to Yewande so that the newcomer would have room. The woman paused, assessing the situation, then turned and motioned silently to someone behind her. A young boy toddled out from behind the shrubs, just as naked as those aboard the lifeboat. His skin and hair shone the color of honey.

She climbed aboard, but the boy needed some help pulling himself up, which Eddie stepped out of the boat to provide. Then Eddie launched the boat and jumped back in once Waniyo had them free. Waniyo rowed vigorously at that point, straight for Oshuna's ship. Yewande smiled and placed her hand on the knee of the woman, who kept looking at Eddie. Eddie flashed a smile but looked away, sensing her discomfort not that he was nude, as were all of them except her, but because of his lighter skin which, even though deeply tanned by that point, could not conceal his European features. A few minutes later when he turned back around, he saw that the woman's shawl had concealed a baby, who was now uncovered and nursing at her breast.

Once they were out in the open surf, Waniyo broke the silence. "*Me llamo Juanillo. ¿Y usted?*"

The new woman responded after a moment's confusion. "*Je m'appelle Marie.*"

The conversation continued, even though, in Eddie's estimation, the two of them were not even speaking the same language. Yewande seemed to understand them both, and translated for Eddie that the boy, named Laurent, was Marie's son, and the baby was her daughter Dominique. Marie had been born enslaved on Saint-Domingue where she grew up, and then she had been sold six years previously to a slave owner who took her to Jamaica and sold her again as soon as they arrived.

Motivated by Yewande's language abilities, Eddie listened attentively to the conversation, thinking he could understand a word every now and again. But the one word that stood out, that he comprehended with absolute clarity, was one he never expected to hear in those circumstances: Hemsworth.

Yewande saw Eddie's open mouth and raised eyebrows. "You know this name?"

"Yes. Can you find out why she mentioned it?"

A few minutes later, Eddie learned what he never would have guessed, but that made a lot of sense: Taylor Hemsworth, Susanna's father, owned a cotton plantation on this island, Jamaica. Hadn't the British recently wrested Jamaica from Spanish rule? Hadn't the Hemsworths recently begun selling cotton by the bolt as well as cotton clothing back in Bristol? Yes, yes, he answered himself, and then his thoughts slid to Susanna. Could there be some chance that she would visit the plantation? Would he be able to see her? Even as Eddie surrendered to this fantasy, blocking out the rest of the foreign conversation around him, he could not help but acknowledge the other immediate circumstance of great interest to him: Yewande had let her right hand settle on his left thigh, where it stayed until they arrived back to the *Ogba*.

Once the group from the rowboat had boarded, Karaya administered the same exam to the newcomers that Eddie had experienced, but without any prolonged attention to their feet or voice. He also could not help but notice that Marie's back was deeply scarred, scored top to bottom from lashes. Karaya rubbed a salve of sunskin onto her back as Oshuna stood watch, holding the baby. Waniyo stayed nearby with the boy, seeming very concerned and protective of Marie.

When Karaya had finished, declaring the three of them to have passed inspection, Oshuna welcomed them aboard and told them they would be arriving at the community the following afternoon. Then she ordered Yewande to take them to get something to eat.

Before Waniyo and Eddie could leave, Oshuna caught Waniyo's attention, motioned with her head toward Eddie, and shrugged her shoulders. Waniyo responded with a nod. Oshuna nodded back, and then he left.

The captain turned to Eddie. "Your labors were acceptable today. Good. Did you form a good team with Yewande?"

Eddie told her about working with Yewande to cut loose the prize oyster, and about the eel. "Why do you need the oysters? To eat?"

"We do eat them, but I need them for the shells. Their insides are coated with nacre, a very important ingredient in the sunskin I make, because it helps heal scars."

"Like Marie's," said Eddie.

"Yes. You helped Marie escape from slavery. Her children, too. Are you aware of this?"

"Yes, captain. I had already guessed it, but it was confirmed by the marks on her back."

"You are now a criminal in the eyes of the slave owners. You know this?"

Eddie nodded.

"Did you ever witness Captain Barlo apply such 'marks,' as you call them, to anyone?"

Eddie shook his head.

"This does not surprise me. For, as you surely saw, he has marks on his own back as well. As do I. Here, look upon me." She turned her back to Eddie. "Tell me what you see."

"I see a row of scars running down from your right shoulder to the bottom left."

"How many scars?"

"They all run together. Too many to count. They form one big scar."

She turned around. "Yes. One big scar. From a malicious man who kept whipping the same spot. What do you think about that, Fife?"

"I think that it is one of the greatest cruelties I have ever seen."

She studied him for a moment. "Let each speak for herself, but as for me, I will not let such cruelty define who I am. Our bodies, Fife… they are our stories, our maps. Karaya, my physic, reads our bodies in her way, and I read them in mine. I look at you, and I see your skill and craft in the calluses on your hands, and your hard work in the strength of your arms and chest. In the way you walk, the way you hold your head, I see your pride. And where you set your eyes is where I see what concerns you. Just as I noted your interest in Yewande, I spied the disgust and sorrow you could not mask when you saw Marie's back. In this way I know you to be decent, to be of kind heart."

As a reflex, Eddie stood as tall as he could and raised his chin. Oshuna laughed.

"At ease, sailor," she said. "You have already proven yourself to me. Don't you see how hard it is to hide, when all you've got on is your own hide?"

Eddie chuckled a little, laughing with Oshuna at her joke. But she quickly stopped.

"I imagine that you do not even know that Marie's son was born to her because she was raped. I ask you again: What do you think about that?"

Eddie set his teeth. "I don't know what to think, but what I feel is rage, and pain… There is too much violence in the world."

Oshuna looked down her nose at Eddie, as if judging, once more, his sincerity. "Yes. Feel for her. Feel for us women. And now look on me and learn a story that must be strange to you as a young man. Look at these heavy breasts that once held milk. Look at these lines on my belly that once marked the growth of its precious treasure. The nacre in the sunskin has helped hide these marks, but I am proud of them, not ashamed of them at all. And you can't see it, but I have a scar running along my keel from bow to stern, from when Yewande was born."

Eddie's skin prickled. "Yewande?"

"Yes, she is my daughter. My only child."

Eddie took a deep breath.

"It is a fact that has no bearing on your relationship to me. I am your captain. And if you and my daughter enjoy each other's company in the way young lovers do, then you have my blessing, because I trust her. And I am learning to trust you."

"Thank you, captain. I would like to ask you a question if I may."

She folded her arms over her chest. "What is your question?"

Eddie swallowed, knowing he couldn't hide the bob of his Adam's apple. "Why did you bring me here?"

Oshuna smiled. "Same reason for you as for Higgins. You are here to work for me."

"But you took Higgins right away. You could have taken me too."

"I had to barter with Barlo. Perhaps you don't understand, Fife, that he wanted to kill you both. You spied on us. We did not know how much of our parley you overheard or understood. I was able to convince him to take you as a crew member, accepting Higgins for my own crew."

"Then you've bartered for me twice, by my count. You seem to have known that Barlo would consider my exchange to the mermaids."

Oshuna winked her left eye. "Some call me the Sea Witch. Like any good sorceress, I will not reveal my secrets. I have told you all that I will."

"Aye, captain."

As Eddie walked away, she began to dance, singing the melody he had heard in Cartagena, *My ship is made a garden, and my ropes are wrought of vine…*

Chapter 10
Another Country

Eddie had slept well in one of the open hammocks. He woke from a dream of pleasure with Bronwen, one of many lately, and it struck him that he no longer dreamed of Susanna. He had made his peace with his distance from Miss Hemsworth, but he was obviously missing Bronwen. Yet here on the *Ogba* with him was a woman who turned his head, and who gave every sign of wanting to know him better. He tried to imagine Yewande turning heads in The White Rose, his favorite tavern back in Bristol, as Susanna had, but immediately he hit a mental block. In the first place, he couldn't imagine a woman of her color in a Bristol tavern. But, more than that, he could not even imagine Yewande dressed at all, let alone dressed the way women did in a British pub. And with that epiphany, he felt his heart go tender: he esteemed her. Her gait, her look, her rare but precise statements—she seemed to him suddenly all the more precious. And still he wondered what to do with so much love, so much desire even as he heard the morning song of his captain, the witch, Yewande's mother. Why had she been so particular about his training with the mermaids, about acquiring him as she had?

He pondered this while humming along with her song. He knew the melody by that point, though not the words in Yoruba. And then, still collecting his wits from the remnants of his dreams, he remembered they would be arriving soon at the community. How often would he hear that song once they were ashore?

It's a lot easier to count your blessings when you don't have many possessions, he thought, as he picked up the belted sheath that Raintree had made for him. Without its knife, the sheath was still useful as a pocket… what a clever and kindly man, that Raintree, he thought. Then he went about his morning chores, just like everybody else was doing, it seemed, except Yewande. He didn't see her anywhere. Higgins told him that she and Waniyo had gone on ahead in the rowboat, to alert the community of their arrival. Eddie felt a little pang of remorse that she hadn't said goodbye to him, as Susanna would have, as Bronwen probably would have. But he quickly dismissed it as a happenstance and got back to trimming the sails.

It was about an hour before dusk when the captain steered the *Ogba* carefully around a small peninsula and into a jagged inlet. Higgins and a few other crew members helped her, along with Waniyo and Yewande who were already ashore. A very rustic dock jutted out from the mangroves, just large and sturdy enough for them to unload. Food and any other items that were to be taken to the community were parceled out among the crew members for transport, and each received an around-the-forehead sling called a tumpline. Eddie found the tumpline odd at first, but soon enough he adjusted the weight to be able to move his back and neck in alignment. Besides, the tumpline was easy to use in comparison to what he saw Yewande and some of the other women doing: with woven rings like crowns, they balanced entire baskets and pots on their heads while stepping gracefully, spilling nothing.

Once everything was secured, Waniyo led the way inland along a path through the mangroves. Oscar the coati ran along with him, on the lookout for snakes, and Onesimus flew overhead. They were followed by Oshuna and half of the crew, then Yewande in the middle, with Marie and her children, just ahead of Eddie, Higgins and the rest of the crew. Karaya brought up the rear.

Eddie could smell dank vegetation in the heavy air. He hadn't been on land for any extended time since living with the mermaids, and their island was relatively arid compared to the humid forest that now enveloped him. Mud squelched around his feet. He had never heard so many birds, monkeys and insects all vocalizing at once. His companions, as they moved under waving branches and leaves, appeared to him as shifting patches of parchment under the mottled light that played over the exuberant expanse of their skin.

"Pay attention," Yewande instructed the newcomers among them, and this was something of an understatement in her usual way, because Eddie, Higgins, and Marie soon observed that the route to the community had been seeded with booby traps: first a camouflaged pit, and then a spring-action net a bit further on. Yewande pointed each of these out without further comment as the procession moved in silence. She took particular care with Marie to ensure that the children stayed out of harm.

It was a half-hour trek uphill through the tropical forest. Eddie was surprised the community hadn't moved even further inland but guessed they had gone just far enough that neither smoke nor sound could reveal their location from the sea. Just as the ground began to slope less dramatically, Eddie saw the wall of trunks that seemed to mark the border of the settlement.

Their arrival had been observed, for when they appeared before the palisade, the gate was already opening. It was a tall portcullis made of sharpened logs that two guards were raising on a pulley system. The group passed through… and entered another country.

Immediately the world exploded into sound. The air, the trees, the ground all throbbed with drumming. Eddie counted a dozen drummers lined up on both sides of the entryway, smacking out a series of syncopated cadences that Oshuna, Yewande and the other regulars recognized. Oshuna swayed her hips and rolled her shoulders to the beat as she led their group into the center of the community, a round open area surrounded by homes of mud and thatch.

The community members, whooping and waving, were gathering around the perimeter of this central circle. No one wore clothing, although plenty of people were adorned with jewelry. The drumming grew louder and faster, stopping only when the entire group of new arrivals was inside the circle. That was the sign for families to reunite: many women and more than a few men rushed forward to welcome back their spouses or siblings or children. There were many hugs and tears of joy.

After a few moments, Oshuna made announcements. She thanked the crew members for another successful voyage aboard the *Ogba*. She thanked the families who had stayed behind for their patience and loyalty. Then she introduced Higgins, Eddie, and Marie with her children as new members of the community. For the time being, she explained, Marie and her children would stay with Karaya, while Eddie would stay with Waniyo, and Higgins with her. Karaya and Waniyo each lived alone, but in their absence, their homes, which Eddie learned to call *bohios*, had been attended to by the members of the community. The newcomers found no spiderwebs, snakes or scorpions in their vacant lodgings, and volunteers quickly strung up hammocks for them.

As the sun was setting, community members lit a bonfire in the circle and prepared a feast of the fresh seafood that the crew had brought up from the ship: spit-roasted crabs, and a fish stew with still more vegetables that Eddie didn't yet know how to name. He stayed at the bonfire long into the night, as did most of the community, a witness to melodies and movements from Africa the likes of which he had never heard nor seen.

***

Eddie awoke early the next morning to the sound of drumming and chanting, but unlike the music of the previous night, it was more subdued and distant. Noticing that Waniyo was gone, he arose nude from the hammock and walked right outside the bohio, never wanting to take for granted the freedom from clothes that he now relished.

He followed the rhythms to a clearing that was some distance away from the houses but still within the palisade that surrounded the community. There he saw Waniyo, who nodded at Eddie while he continued drumming. In the middle of the clearing were Yewande, Oshuna, Marie and two other women. They were raking lines with hoes—many parallel lines close together—and they had almost finished scoring all the ground in the clearing.

When she saw him, Oshuna called out, "Come help us sow, Fife!"

He looked around the clearing. The women were nude, with neither bags nor baskets. They had no containers for storing anything. "Glad to help," Eddie replied. "Where are the seeds?"

Oshuna gave her hoe to her daughter, signaling all the women to put their implements away. Then she approached Eddie as she spoke to him. "There are a great many things you do not know. But I will admit that there are a great many things I do not know, either. This is why I say, let me share with you, so that I may also let you share with me. We build what we know as we go along together, yes?"

Eddie nodded.

Oshuna nodded back. "Then let me share with you the dance of the seeds."

Clutching his shoulders, she pushed him gently backward a few paces until he stood under a tree. When she had returned to the middle of the clearing, she and Yewande and the other women held their arms out to their sides and leaned forward. Waniyo accelerated into a new rhythm, and the women began to dance while shaking their heads, sending their shoulders and arms into fantastic undulations. Out sprung the seeds, like fountains… from their hair. There were so many shapes and sizes and colors of seeds, and they went flying all over the ground, scattered willy-nilly. Eddie was astonished that so many seeds could have been stored in the curls and kinks of their marvelous hair.

The five dancers were smiling, shimmying their shoulders, stopping sometimes to squat and urinate a bit, to both fix and nourish the seeds. The whole time, Oshuna was intoning a chant meant to bless the sowing. The gold-and-pearl pendants she wore that day swung freely from her ears, and a cowrie necklace shook and crashed against her swaying breasts.

After a while, she called out to Eddie. "Don't just stand about, Fife! Stop gaping and gawking, and come piss on the ground with us, at least!"

And so he did, since by that point he was about as uninhibited as he could imagine regarding his body and its functions. He hopped from spot to spot, spurting urine like a cur marking its turf. And when the women had run their fingers through their hair, and found no more seeds to be flung, the six of them kept dancing and hopping and stomping, and Waniyo kept drumming, all for good measure that the seeds would sprout and bring abundant harvest.

When they finally stopped, Oshuna laughed with satisfaction. "You were surprised, eh, Fife? Where are those seeds coming from, you asked yourself, yes? Ah, but this is an old secret, an ancient practice of my people. For those of us who broke free from slavery, this secret has brought us life."

"It is a truly amazing secret," said Eddie. "What seeds have we just sown?"

Yewande answered. "Sorghum and millet. Yams, okra, wild onion, the kola nut tree, the coffee bush, garvance. We trade for them, but we also collect them from what we harvest from the garden on the *Ogba*, and we can take back to the *Ogba* the seeds we need from here. Did you know *ogba* means garden?"

"I do now," Eddie said.

"These are the gifts of my people, the gifts of my land," added Oshuna. "We spread them here in this place that some people call the New World, though it is just as old as any other. And we mix with them some of the seeds from this land: pumpkin and squash, beans and corn and chilies. Marie brought many of these when she escaped. Imagine, Fife: an entire garden ready to sprout from her head but hidden in plain sight."

Marie made a joke in her language that Yewande explained: perhaps Eddie could smuggle seeds in his beard. Eddie stroked his beard self-consciously. It had grown quite a bit, but it was not all that long, which explained the prolonged laughter from the group.

Yewande locked her eyes on his. "Beard or no beard, Eddie, I'm sure you have a garden ready to sprout inside that head of yours."

He bowed slightly. "Whatever good may come from it, is yours to harvest."

The air was suddenly filled with the shouts of children. Karaya had arrived, escorting Laurent and Dominique, Marie's children, along with a few more kids, and she exchanged them, as it were, for Eddie. Eddie noticed that Waniyo smiled broadly when Laurent ran to him. He already seemed to be forming a family with Marie.

"Learn from Karaya, Fife," said Oshuna. "We need you for this."

Eddie had no idea what was going on, but he nodded to Oshuna, winked at Yewande, smiled at the children, and followed Karaya as she led him from the clearing.

Karaya seemed to be the oldest person in the community, but she was still quite spry, and her long, braided hair swished briskly back and forth all the way down her back and over her bottom as she led Eddie out beyond the community wall. After a brief walk to the west, they stopped at a large boulder.

"Remember how I looked at your feet? When you first came to the *Ogba*. And I had you sing with me?"

Eddie nodded.

"Here is where you need them—your feet and your voice—for learning the song map. This song I learned from my grandmother. Listen."

She began to sing a simple melody with no words. Nodding and gesturing, she encouraged Eddie to join her as she sang through the two phrases of the melody another three times.

"Now," she said, "look at the rocks."

She pointed at the landscape, and Eddie did not understand what she meant until she began walking from one vegetation-covered lump to another. As they moved over an area of some twenty-five yards, she pointed out all the "rocks," even though some were not rocks but logs.

Then she stopped. "Each rock is a part of the song. I show you."

They walked back to the first rock. She stood on it and sang the first note, then pointed to another rock and sang the second note. She jumped to that rock and sang the second note again. The third rock, Eddie could see, was quite close to the second, and as she jumped to it, he noticed the interval between the second and third notes was also close. He began to understand that the notes of the song indicated the distance between the rocks.

Soon he was jumping and singing along behind her. Some of the jumps were quite challenging, for both of them.

One of the leaps near the end was particularly far, and it lined up with a big jump in the notes of the melody.

They made it through. "Now we go again," Karaya said.

Eddie accompanied her back to the beginning, and as they sang and jumped all the way through once more, he discovered another aspect of the melody: a repeated note meant that the next leap was straight ahead. If the pitch rose, then the next leap was to the right, and if it fell, the leap was to the left.

Karaya, only slightly out of breath at the end of the course, began to say "Now we go…"

"Wait," Eddie interrupted. "Why? What is the purpose of this?"

"I placed these rocks," she said. "I need you, and Oshuna too, we need you to know this song map, because we will take it where it goes."

Eddie pondered this, looking back and forth between Karaya and the landscape she had arranged. "This is a practice course," he guessed. "We're preparing to do this somewhere else—a place where the song matches the way you set out these rocks."

Karaya nodded and headed back to start again. "The place where the song matches is dark," she added as Eddie caught up to her. She found a stick on the ground and gave it to him, saying "We hold fire."

Eddie smiled. "A practice torch. I see. Is that all?"

"Wet," she said. "Wet rocks in the dark. Must not fall."

Eddie's smile faded abruptly.

After another five times jumping through the course with the substitute torches, Karaya told Eddie they were done for the day. "Tomorrow we come at night and jump with fire," she added.

Eddie felt exhausted. By the time they returned to the community, the sun had set. Karaya disappeared inside her bohio.

Yewande was using a long stick to stir the fire in the middle of the central circle. She beckoned Eddie to join her. As he sat next to her, he pointed at a clay pot partially buried in the embers. "What's in there?"

"A surprise," said Yewande. Then she pointed at Eddie's heart. "Do you have any surprises in there?"

Eddie chuckled and shook his head. "You and your mother—you both seem very interested in who and how I love. Why is that?'

"Are you sure you want to know?"

"I don't understand why you would ask that, but yes, I am sure."

Yewande sighed. "My mother had a dream. Years ago when I was just a girl. In the dream she saw me in the future, as a mother, with a child. She said that what most struck her about the dream was the radiant golden light all around me, and this light was love. She could not see the child's father, but she knew that the father was also in the light, maybe the source of the light. You see, my mother has the idea that not everyone knows how to truly love, or even cares to learn. She thinks the child is important, somehow, for the future. A portent, she called it, born from love. You know she fancies herself a witch, someone who can understand a dream like that." She paused, stirring the fire. "And then, well I haven't told you, but I had a husband."

Eddie's eyebrows shot up. "You were married?"

"As officially as possible, the way we do marriages here in the community. His name was Amadi. As tall as you, as handsome as you, as smart as you, but black like me."

"What happened?"

"There are many things I could tell you that happened. For now, I will say that he was killed by slave catchers. That was two years ago."

Eddie swallowed hard and reached for her hand. "I'm so sorry, Yewande."

"I believe that you are sorry, Eddie." She clasped his hand in both of hers. "And so does Amadi. He… talks to me. You could say his spirit is still in contact with mine."

"You are an incredible woman."

"Thank you, Eddie. Sometimes I believe it. Amadi held the same opinion, and he is very jealous of me. But, when I speak with him over there at the ceiba tree, he approves of you. And my mother does too. And, most importantly of all, I approve of you."

"I am humbled."

"My mother thought Amadi must have been the father that she could not see in the dream. But now she thinks it is you. When she first saw you, you impressed her in body and spirit, both. And the locket you had—she decided that the locket meant that you are capable of loving."

Eddie exhaled heavily. "So this is the reason for so much bartering back and forth, with Captain Barlo, with the mermaids?"

Yewande nodded. "It is as you say."

Eddie picked up the stick and poked at the fire. "What about you? What do you make of it?"

"I love my mother, but I don't always understand her. If all of this is so important to her, then I don't understand why she won't tell me more about my own father, or what happened to him." She looked down. "The child? If it were just a matter of childbearing, then I wouldn't even be asking you about your heart and what's in it. I'd just like to know… I'm not sure, but I think I love…"

The explosion had Eddie on his feet in an instant. "Move!" he yelled. When Yewande stayed seated, he tried to lift her from behind, pulling her up until he realized she was laughing.

Completely confused, Eddie stared again at the pot in the embers, which seemed to be in a state of perpetual agitation. "Is that… some kind of witch's magic?"

"Yes," Yewande said, laughing so hard she could hardly breathe, tears streaming down her nose. "Oh, yes, it is magic indeed… Please, sit down, I will show you."

After waiting a few moments for the explosions to subside, she used the poking stick to fish the pot from the fire by its handle. She licked her fingers before quickly sweeping the lid off the pot.

Eddie looked inside. "It looks like… puffs of clouds. And it smells delicious."

Yewande gingerly pinched a piece and put it in her mouth. Eddie heard the crunch. Then she held a piece out for him, and he opened his mouth. He had never tasted such a crispy lightness. "What is it?"

"Popcorn," said Yewande. "Karaya taught us how to make it. It's a favorite of mine."

"I'm so hungry," Eddie said, plunging his hand into the fluffy kernels and bringing a fistful to his mouth all at once. "You know, I could learn to like this," he added, forcing the words through his full mouth.

Yewande laughed again, and it was the biggest smile he had ever seen on her. She reached her hand full of popcorn, and tried to eat some more, but she was still laughing, and so she spilled some, and a piece got caught in her pubic hair, which made her laugh even more. Just from her laughing, Eddie laughed so hard his abdomen hurt.

Yewande stopped quickly and suddenly.

"Oh! You do that just like your mother," Eddie observed, trying to get serious.

"Eddie," she said, "right when the corn started popping, I was telling you… that I think I love you."

Eddie looked away, then reached for more popcorn.

Yewande stayed his hand. "You need to say something to me now."

He looked her straight in the eyes. "Yewande, I think I love you too. And so I want you to know that I've been saying that a lot lately."

He held out his left palm, then placed a kernel of popcorn in it with his right hand. "Before I left home—it's been nineteen months now—I told Susanna I loved her. She is the one who gave me the locket your mother saw."

Placing another kernel in his palm, he continued. "Just five days ago, I told Bronwen, the mermaid, that I loved her."

Yewande placed a third kernel in his hand before he had the chance. "Yes," he said, "and now you've told me that you think you love me, too."

Yewande did not break eye contact. "Eddie, you have such a noble heart for telling me this truth. I do not ask you to choose. If so much love is in your heart, then accept all of it." As she spoke, she fed Eddie the three kernels, one by one. "It is hard to eat just one kernel. Far better to let the heat and light of love set off many explosions. Let there be more love."

Chapter 11
Mother of Pearl

Eddie walked out of Waniyo's bohio the next morning and headed toward the circle. Laurent and several other children of varying ages and skin tones were running and playing near the massive ceiba, the tallest tree inside the community walls. Some adults were preparing food over the fire. Others were training: some were leaping and stretching, and some, holding staffs, practiced duels that seemed almost like dances.

Everyone was naked, and very much by choice. What need for clothing here?

The Hemsworths... and their cotton, Eddie thought. People—just like the people around him, just like people everywhere—had been enslaved, brutalized, treated like property, all to cut sugarcane, to pick cotton, and so many other grueling tasks... the cotton to make the clothes that he now saw to be so often unnecessary. He could recall the citizens of Bristol trying to outdo each other in their finery, ignorant of the crimes behind every stitch—as he had been— ignorant of the evil their clothing cloaked... ignorant... Susanna, and so many others, living in such vast ignorance, as unaware of the price of slavery as were the enslaved harvesters of cacao unfamiliar with the flavor of chocolate. But what did Mr. Hemsworth know?

Eddie joined the group leaping, stretching, swinging the staff, all to the beat of a gourd drum that incited him to focus, to assert his lived truths, to contemplate fighting for the right to be free. It did not take long for him to feel stronger, more balanced. With each thrust and squat and parry, he knew that fighting for freedom was well worth it, and fighting alongside the community, an honor.

During his leaping and parrying, Yewande returned from the *Ogba*, where she had carried a pot of fresh water to flush out the splashed seawater from the garden over the poop deck. As usual, she walked with admirable equilibrium, balancing the large pot effortlessly atop her head. Eddie fell in with her and followed her to the central circle. As she began crushing together some garlic and basil, he asked her which herbs she had collected and what purposes they had.

Yewande opened the lid of her pot, now filled with a variety of leaves, bark, and roots. "These herbs are not just for cooking. They are the elements of a game my mother is always playing. She's been playing it as long as I can remember. She started me in helping her when I was very young, because it was just the two of us—nobody else to look after me. The game, or the challenge, is to make the best possible sunskin. She is always refining her recipe, and tonight we will be mixing a batch with a new herb—these ones here, the leaves of the ackee. Some of these herbs have no name in English, or even Yoruba, but only Taino. Why not make use of whatever she can? She tells me that her most important dreams are always about this game. And if I laugh, or tease, she reminds me that the sunskin protects us all that we may live without clothing. She reminds me also that the sunskin is our most significant item for trade."

Eddie picked up an ackee leaf and sniffed it. "It would seem you are the most trusted source, at least for Barlo and his crew, and the mermaids. When she changes the recipe, how does she test it?"

"Look at my back. Have you noticed?"

Yewande turned, but Eddie could see nothing unusual.

"Do you see the two moons?"

She angled her back into the sun, and in the middle of the right side of her back Eddie saw a circle of skin, about the size of a large coin, that was slightly lighter in color than the skin around it. He touched a finger to it.

"I see this one. Where is the other one?"

"Directly opposite, on the left. It will be harder to see."

Eddie scrutinized her other side, and with the precise knowledge of where to look, he was able to see it: a circle of the same size, slightly darker than the surrounding skin. He touched it.

"What are they?"

"This is how she tests her mixes. Whenever she adjusts the recipe, she puts some on a little wooden disk and presses it against my back. It is her quest for perfection."

Eddie stroked his chin. "So, this one, on the left, was not an effective mix."

Yewande turned to face him. "I can't see them, so I don't know. But yes, my mother said the same thing about that side."

Eddie recalled the motif of two equal-sized circles next to each other. "The flag she flies on the *Ogba*... this is the design! I never knew what it meant."

"It's more of a happy accident than any deliberate plan. My mother wanted the circles on the flag to be able to represent many twinned circles on our bodies."

Eddie nodded, thinking. "Eyes? Nipples?"

Yewande held her arms out in front of her with her hands doubled back toward her face.

Eddie laughed. "Elbows!"

"Yes! And knees and heels," she added, "and thumbs and big toes, and of course breasts and buttocks and ballocks, and many others."

Eddie smiled at these parallels. "And also 'O' for Oshuna and 'O' for *Ogba*. Your mother is a very... unique person."

"I know it. Sometimes I call her Mother of Pearl, because that's another name for the nacre from the oysters we collect. And yet for me she is also very normal. Just my mother. She told me she was amazed to learn how many ways there are to say eyes, for example, or breasts, when she was learning English, in addition to all the ways she knew in Yoruba. It made her want something that could be a symbol outside of language."

Eddie reached around her to press his thumbs into the circles on her back. "Every time I see the flag, I will think of your back."

Yewande kissed him. "Just my back?"

"And your eyes," he responded as he kissed each one. "And your… all of you."

After a long embrace, Eddie let Yewande continue her work, and he found Waniyo to apprentice with him as he had done aboard the *Ogba*. They replaced some planks in the perimeter fence, raked the central circle, and cleaned out the fire pit. As the sun was setting, they had just begun putting together a new barrel when Karaya approached them, carrying a pair of torches.

"It's time, Eddie. We must practice the song in the dark."

He rose and accepted a torch. There was only a sliver of moon, and it was very dark by the time they reached the course Karaya had constructed. The night chorus of frogs, birds, monkeys, and insects made the singing more difficult than during the day, but Karaya told him they would not have to contend with those particular animals on the actual stone path. The two of them jumped through the path many times, until they could do it without dropping the torches, and even without singing out loud.

***

When they returned to the community, a guard whistled low and loud, and then motioned for Eddie to take his place in the central circle, where it seemed the entire community had gathered, standing around the periphery facing out. In the middle of the circle stood Oshuna and Yewande; Karaya joined them there. A pot hung over the fire. Eddie sidled in between Waniyo and Higgins and turned his back to the fire.

"What are we doing?"

"*Es un secreto*," said Waniyo.

"Keeping the secret," said Higgins. "They're making the sunskin."

"They have all the ingredients now?" Eddie turned to look.

"Stay still," whispered Higgins. "We were told not to look into the circ…"

"What's the consternation?" rang the voice of Oshuna.

"*Nada, señora*," responded Waniyo, adding an insistent *shhh* to Eddie and Higgins.

As they stood in silence, they heard the grinding of mortar and pestle, punctuated by the conversation of the three women—not always in English—as ingredients were called for and measured. Eddie knew that Yewande had been extracting the nacre by soaking the oyster shells in vinegar and scraping their interiors. In her daily visits to the *Ogba* to tend the potted plants and garden, she had been harvesting what she needed, and from the community garden as well: aloe, prickly pear cactus, okra, lavender, basil, ginger, rose, and coconut oil. The latter, he remembered her saying, had to be processed specifically from the coconuts that had been used as hanging planters for the aloe.

Eddie pictured, in his mind's eye, the graceful sway of Yewande's shoulders and hips in the act of stirring the pot, and just as he was beginning to feel aroused by his desire for her, he heard her start to chant. Her voice lilted and lingered in the low register, singing to him, seeming to be summoning him—Eddie, only him—its pitches and rhythms tickling his ears and winding all the way up his legs like tendrils. The hair on his arms and legs stood on end.

Eddie turned not only his head but his entire body around, irresistibly. Yewande's voice had enthralled him, his arms and penis lifting into the air even as his feet began shuffling toward her. He was bewitched. Waniyo shook his head and backed up quickly, always keeping his face away from the sunskin makers, moving backwards while trying to catch up to Eddie to detain him, but it was too late. Just as Eddie was about to reach them, Oshuna gave a great cry, high and long and loud. The enchantment broke.

"Come," said Yewande as she took Eddie's hand. He was unaware of having moved to the middle of the circle.

"Karaya, please continue with the sunskin," Oshuna ordered. "The rest of you stay put... except you, Higgins. Come with us."

Oshuna led her daughter and the two Englishmen to her bohio. Once they were inside, she gave Eddie a cup of cold water.

"This was a test, Eddie. Yewande's voice entranced you. It confirms what I suspected when I first saw you, knocked out on the dock with your locket: it wasn't so much that you were a man in love, as that you were a man capable of loving. You already love Yewande—her voice alone was enough to enchant you, but only you. No one else responded as you did.

"Eddie, I left Tokunbo because love had left him. His pains, his grief, his anger—all of it had swallowed his capacity to love. I did not want the same fate for my daughter."

Eddie sipped some water, then shook his head and pinched his arms, still coming out of the trance. "Who is Tokunbo?"

"He was my lover. We met just before we stepped on that cage of horror, the *Mercy*. Sijuwola was there, too, and many other people from our communities. I think it would be difficult for you to imagine, Eddie, what a great and wicked evil it is to be sold by your own people—uprooted from your land and from your family—and then stuffed into the hold of a ship, stacked like one more catch."

Eddie looked away. "I've heard…"

"No."

"I've read…"

"No, no! You must accept—Eddie, listen to me—you must accept that this is something you simply cannot know. Imagine? Yes. Please, try to imagine. You will not come close, but try to imagine, to feel what it would be like. For that is the best you can do."

Eddie stared at her intently, finally responding with just a nod.

"We could not move. They barely fed us," Oshuna began, with a long exhalation after each statement. "Everyone was sick. There was such a stench. So many died. Some of them were tossed to sea. Others were left to rot right next to us. I wanted to breathe, and there was no breath. I wanted to shout, and there was no voice. I was barely alive only because I was not completely dead." Oshuna took Eddie's hands in hers. "Please imagine."

Eddie released a long exhalation to match hers. He closed his eyes for a few moments and struggled to visualize such cruelty.

"A storm came," she continued. "There was only one man on that wretched ship that truly showed any mercy. Peter. He could no longer abide the horrors he had seen on board. In the thick of the storm, while the slavers were all busy, Tokunbo and Sijuwola escaped, and when Peter saw this, he helped them set a few others free, and helped those men overcome the captain and crew. Then they set us all free. My skin was oozing pus and blood. My eyes were swollen. My bones felt like they did not remember how to be bones. But the air, Eddie, and the splash of the waves. I had never felt freedom so keenly.

"By that point, it did not even matter to me that I was naked to the elements. When the slavers had ripped the clothing from us, just before chaining us together and marching us onto the *Mercy*—yes, that was one more insult that made me cry out in the unspeakable terror of what was happening to us. But in the moment that I was freed—and it was Tokunbo who undid the chains, and he was also naked—I only knew the relief of movement. Not until much later did I think about how being naked is a powerful freedom that enhances relief, that enhances movement."

Eddie nodded, vaguely aware that Yewande must have been listening to a story she had heard many times before. Higgins seemed to be familiar with some of it already, as well.

"Tokunbo wanted to kill the crew of the *Mercy*, or else throw them overboard. Peter and Sijuwola and I convinced him to set them adrift in the rowboats instead. We distributed all the remaining provisions equally to each of the thirty people left on board and set about tending to our many wounds and nourishing ourselves as best we could. Then, we began to learn from Peter. How to run the ship, how to navigate, the rigging, the sails, the anchor—all of it. And we learned how to speak his language, English. We sang, we listened to stories with lines that we repeated. He was a very good teacher. And he decided that since none of us had any clothes, then he would not wear any, either. His white skin burned severely, though, and that was when I started thinking about sunskin.

"We stayed at sea as long as we could. When we made it to San Juan, the men hatched a plan to trade the *Mercy* for another ship. It was smaller and faster and did not hold the memories of terror that we all still felt. Most of the people who had survived the journey with us stayed in Puerto Rico, but I went with Tokunbo, because we had begun to love each other.

"But as I told you, love left Tokunbo. He grew a love with me at first, but then all he could talk about was revenge, and hatred, and rancor. I was trying to love, to forgive… and so I left him after only a few months. One night when he was planning with Sijuwola and Peter, I waited until they had passed out from their rum, and then I escaped on the lifeboat. I knew that I was expecting Tokunbo's child, as much as I knew I wanted a better home for her.

"I made that home for a while on St. Kitts. That's where I met Karaya—she was my midwife when Yewande was born. Then Karaya and I started making sunskin. We sold enough to the pale-skinned Brits and French on the island that eventually I was able to purchase my own ship. The *Mercy* was a ship of death, but I made the *Ogba*, my dear garden, into a ship of life.

"And so I dedicated myself to rescuing people who, like me, decided to escape from slavery. Many of them have become my crew. Most of the others live here in the community. And I kept an ear out for news. I learned that Peter died in a skirmish with a Dutch ship… but it has been a long time without news of anyone named Tokunbo."

"Yewande was born on St. Kitts?" Eddie asked.

"Yes," Oshuna answered, turning toward her daughter. "She is a child of the Caribbean. Karaya is, too—she was born near here. But of course Tokunbo and I were born in Africa – he in Owo and I in Osogbo, not too far apart."

"Higgins and I were both born in Bristol, England."

"Yes," the captain nodded. "Listen, Eddie. One thing we all have in common is that we were all born naked—vulnerable, for better or for worse. We were born exposed and open to the world, and I think it is better to stay that way."

"I agree," said Higgins. "From what I've seen, being naked doesn't eliminate violence or cruelty, but it can weaken them, and lessen their frequency."

"You've seen," added Oshuna, "that our community is open to anybody, of any color or age or background, who is willing to live with the freedom, but also the vulnerability, of nudity. We have grown in love, in our capacity to love each other, because we recognize our shared vulnerability."

"I'm in," said Eddie. "This is my home now, if you'll have me."

"Mine, too," said Higgins.

Oshuna opened her arms wide. "Yes, you are welcome to stay, of course."

"Please stay," said Yewande, with her biggest smile and a tight embrace for Eddie.

Chapter 12
The Cove of Spirits

Two figures set out in a rowboat under the darkness of a new moon. A pair of lit torches affixed to the sides of the boat revealed their presence, but Karaya had explained to Eddie that there was no way to light the torches once they arrived at their destination, a cove that carved into an island two miles across the open water from the community.

Eddie had imagined the domed cove many times based on Karaya's descriptions. Still, he had not anticipated the way the torchlight bounced off the water, the way it lit up a diminishing sliver along the rock wall, or how the roll of the surf sounded once they were under the cave-like roof. They moored the boat to the first and largest of the rocks, just visible above the low tide. Then Eddie nervously reached for his belted sheath—his pocket—for the last of the jerky Yewande had given him. Torch in hand, he surveyed what he could see of the cove's interior, hoping to catch something that Karaya might have overlooked on her numerous visits here, but he could only confirm what she had already told him: there was no space to walk along the edge of the cove, and its walls were too slick to climb. There was no place else to leave the boat, even though it was visible here from outside. He sighed in resignation. The only approach lay before them, over the steppingstones whose positions Karaya had so carefully recreated to train Eddie, but whose slippery, almost submerged surfaces were much more dangerous than the practice course.

Most daunting were the dots of light Eddie could see just above the surface of the water, reflecting back to him in the torchlight. The dots did not move, but Karaya had warned him that their owners moved quickly.

"Yes," Karaya affirmed, guessing his thoughts. "Those are eyes of crocodiles. Don't drop torch."

Eddie squeezed his torch tight.

"With hurry," said Karaya. "Remember what I show you. With hurry, with balance."

Eddie nodded, and she had already hopped gracefully to the next stone, torch held high. After one more leap, she turned back, waiting for him to make his first jump. This would be their system, since only one person at a time could barely fit on each stone. Eddie took a few moments longer than Karaya liked, but in that brief time he set himself back into the frame of mind of all the practicing they had done at the community. When he did leap, he landed confidently, and Karaya even managed a smile. Then she hopped on ahead, and he followed, and it seemed to him, as they got into a rhythm, that they had been jumping for a long time without getting much closer to the back of the cove.

Karaya hummed to remember where the next stone was, and Eddie brimmed with renewed respect for her, and her people, for such an ingenious method—the way the notes of the melody formed a map in her mind, so that even here in the darkness, she could remember in which direction, and how far, to leap to the next stone. He easily understood why, as she had told him, it was better to have at least two people with the ability to get to the back of the cove.

After Eddie's next leap, Karaya paused instead of moving forward immediately. Eddie guessed that they were about three-quarters in, at the particularly difficult leap. She continued humming, repeating a certain part of the melody, and then stopped to take a deep breath. On these slippery, small surfaces, there was no room for a running start. She turned to her left and swung her arms, her torch illuminating a wide arc of the darkened cove. And jumped.

In the flash of her torchlight, Eddie saw them. Two, or was it three, black shapes scissoring the air behind her—

something threw her off, and she landed poorly, splashing into the water and dropping her torch, which extinguished immediately.

Eddie's skin crawled as the horror washed over him like the now rising tide: by the light of his torch, he saw the bats spinning crazily all around them, pouring out of the back of the cove toward the entrance. And he saw, too, the approach of the eyes of the crocodiles, alerted by Karaya's splash.

"Karaya!"

"Eddie! My leg! Bad!"

Eddie swallowed hard and turned back around. "What can I do?"

"You must jump this stone and next, quickly, so I can get out water onto this one."

"But I can't even see the stone you jumped from!"

Eddie heard some ripples, and for a few anguished moments, he had no idea what was happening.

"I swim! Bad!"

Eddie understood she had swum back to his next stone.

"Right. Can you wave your hand?"

At the very end of his torchlight's reach, Eddie could make out a back-and-forth movement that must have been her hand.

"I see you!"

"Now I am my hands pointing stone."

Eddie took a deep breath. "What if the bats make me fall, too? We could wait until they all get out."

"No! No wait!" Karaya yelled as loudly as she could. "Water rises! Crocodiles!"

Eddie heard sudden splashes to his right, and he spun so quickly he almost lost his balance. Whatever it was, he missed it, but a few seconds later it happened again, and this time, he saw: a crocodile launched its front end, heavy but powerful, into the air with jaws wide open, and caught a bat that had come too close to the water. Eddie saw the jagged end of a wing, sticking out between the endless teeth, twist and disappear as the massive lizard began to chew and swallow.

"With hurry!" came her cry. Then, "You are strong, Eddie! I need you!"

Eddie understood the bats could at least help keep the crocodiles occupied, but he didn't know how much longer their exodus would last. He had never felt so vulnerable, so exposed… and yet he wanted to believe Karaya, to believe that he was strong. He composed himself, and concentrated, and jumped. Slipping only slightly, he landed close to where Karaya's hands had been.

"Where are you?" he called out. Hearing ripples, he understood she was already moving back to the stone where she fell. Soon he heard her call his name again, and then, even more tenuously than before, he saw what he thought to be her hands waving.

This was the longest, most difficult jump, and Karaya, who had done it many times before, had failed. Eddie knew his chance at success was grim, but he had no option. If he abandoned her, to return to the boat, he'd never find the steppingstones on his own, and he'd fall to his fate. More importantly, he knew in his deepest core that he would not, could not, abandon her. To do so would be against his understanding of honor. He had to leap into the darkness, into the danger.

Quickly he hummed through the melody, with its relative pitches so vital to get right. He pictured himself back at the community, on the practice course, and then he focused on coordinating his legs with his ears, in the sense of adjusting his jump to the interval. Into the void, before he could lose the location of the spot where he had seen Karaya's hands, he jumped.

It was a hard landing. He had nailed the trajectory but overestimated his force. He scraped knees and shins and dropped his torch on impact, but it stayed put, and in its light Eddie detected movement. There was a colony of crabs on that rock whose sheer numbers had detained the torch. They crawled from the light slowly, as if they had been in a state of torpor.

Brandishing the flame, he looked out toward the sound of splashing. To get out of his way, Karaya had decided to swim to the next rock. But in the beam from the torch, what he saw was not Karaya.

"Hurry!" he yelled hoarsely, as his body responded quicker than his thoughts. There were a few quick pinches, but the urgency of the moment overrode any pain from the claws as he scooped crab after crab and pelted them at the crocodile, who stopped in confusion and then submerged. Eddie continued throwing crabs in the area, realizing the crocodile would detect their movements in the water and gobble them up like pellets.

It was enough time. Karaya emerged onto the next rock. Before jumping, Eddie chucked more crabs further and further out, to lead the menace away from his trajectory. Karaya jumped blind to the next rock and called out that she had made it. In a moment, Eddie went back through the song and made his jump.

Success. For Eddie, there were just two more rocks, three more leaps in total. Karaya quickly jumped to the last rock. Eddie matched her speed to land confidently on the rock she had just occupied.

"Remember ledge!" yelled Karaya, who leaped and landed deliberately in the water just short of the narrow ledge. In the dim light, Eddie saw her pull herself up and shimmy along, one foot after the other, to a slightly wider area.

Eddie was about to jump when he heard Karaya yell, "Again!" He didn't understand her until he turned and saw a telltale pair of eyes below him in the torchlight. He scanned the rock: no crabs here—all he saw were his own bleeding shins and knees. He'd just have to jump anyway.

He looked out into the murk again to see if the crocodile had moved. It hadn't. Eddie began to turn into his leap when he heard a colossal wet whoosh and turned back just in time to see the crocodile thrashing in the wide-open jaws of a shark. Eddie could not look away from the spectacle. The dueling beasts roiled the water, splashing and spinning one over the other, churning the entire cove, but it was over quickly. The shark plunged into the depths with its prey, leaving an eerie stillness.

His body covered in goosebumps, Eddie shook his head to focus. He jumped to the last rock. Then, just as they had practiced, he threw the torch to Karaya, and jumped short of the ledge to pull himself out. One torch down, and plenty of bruises, but they'd made it.

Eddie pointed to Karaya's injured leg. "That looks bad."

She shrugged. "Seawater heal. Also, my blood bring shark."

Eddie nodded. "I bet you're right. Did you see it?"

"Could not see, only hear. And feel. Come this way, we are close."

They skirted along the narrow verge of the back of the cove and came into a sandy area with archways of rock, some quite large, others more like very short tunnels, and still others that were quite small. Karaya led Eddie around one of the arches to a cluster of debris—it was the shipwreck she had told him was blocking whatever it was she needed to get. It looked like a fishing boat had gotten caught at high tide and slammed into the back of the cove.

Eddie felt exhausted already but understood there was nothing to do but start moving logs and beams. He found a steady spot to leave the torch burning upright. They propped the smaller logs against the back wall of the cove. It took both of them to lift several of the larger beams and move them to one side. Squatting and lifting opposite Karaya, Eddie became conscious that even though he had adapted to constant nudity, there was still some level in which he found the entire situation so completely improbable as to seem like a dream.

Finally they had cleared enough away to access a crude niche carved into the rock wall. The niche was covered by spider webs that Eddie severed with his knife. Tiny black spiders fell on his arms and chest, but most dropped immediately to the ground. Eddie brushed the remaining few away easily, with help from Karaya who blew some of them off his shoulders. Karaya smiled, reaching into the niche to remove a scrap of hide with some writing on it. "Speak it," she said, passing it to Eddie. "Words from Oshuna."

Eddie raised his eyebrows. "Oshuna was here?"

"Only once. She say she never come again."

"I'm not surprised," he said with a bitter chuckle, deducing that his potential ability to learn the cove's leaps was yet another reason Oshuna had bartered for him as a healthy young man.

He spread out the hide and read aloud: "*'Ere you dare to touch my lair, your mind, your soul, your body bare.*"

Eddie laughed, considering that he and Karaya were completely bare except for her amulet and his belted sheath.

"Is not to laugh, Eddie. These spiders, they dropped to the ground right away because you are bare. But the man who cuts through these webs wearing clothes, he will have angry hungry spiders hiding and biting until he gets bare, like he should have in the first place."

Eddie raised his eyebrows in renewed amazement of life without clothes.

Karaya was removing something from the niche that looked like a bundle the size of an infant. "Zemi," she said, and turned it so that Eddie could see it in the torchlight. It was an effigy made of heavy cotton and wood, depicting an ancient-looking female figure, seated, nude, with large eyes and mouth. Her arms were curved in front of her, and there was a high level of artisanal detail in her fingers and toes, her teeth, her nipples and vulva.

"Grandmother of grandmothers," said Karaya. "Protect." She intoned a brief hymn, touching her face and the zemi's face repeatedly. Then she handed the zemi to Eddie. "She has bones. Many spirits. No dropping zemi."

The word *zemi* rolled around inside Eddie's memory, jiggling and triggering a memory of uncertain provenance… until he recalled it was the word he had heard Barlo and Oshuna repeat so frequently on the dock that foggy evening in Cartagena.

Karaya had reached further back into the niche, and this time she pulled out a small chest and set it on the sand. She opened it, and the contents of the chest glittered in the torchlight: coins, jewels, a pair of golden goblets, sparkling necklaces. Eddie finally felt a sense of accomplishment for all the training and jumping, for enduring the bruised legs and menacing beasts.

Just as he was wondering how they would transport the chest, he saw that Karaya was sifting through all the treasure to the bottom. She pulled out a pouch on a chain, slipped it over her head, and closed the chest, leaving everything else inside.

"Wait," said Eddie, looking at the pouch, which was about the size of his fist. "That's it? We're leaving the rest of it here?"

"Very safe," responded Karaya, pushing the chest to the back of the niche.

Eddie supposed he could not disagree. "What's in the bag?"

Karaya took the zemi back from him and replaced it in the niche, as far back as she could push it out of sight. "Gold," she said simply. "For sunskin."

"Gold," Eddie repeated. "Gold dust?"

"The Spaniards, they ask for gold from my ancestors. My ancestors would tell them, go to next island. And on the next island, the people would say, oh, it's the next island, keep going, and it went on and on like that here in this ocean."

Eddie nodded. "Kind of like the steppingstones. Clever."

Karaya shook her finger at Eddie. "Not clever. Those Spanish people going from island to island, they spread their sickness and kill almost all my people. Who they did not kill from sickness, they kill other ways."

"That's horrible," said Eddie, not knowing what else to say.

"Yes. Horrible," Karaya repeated. "Is what made me want to learn healing. And made me sad that I could not heal the sickness they brought to these islands."

Eddie looked at the fresh wound on Karaya's leg, just starting to scar. He knew she would have a salve to apply to it once they returned. Then he looked out into the dark cove, where he could make out the faintest bit of moonlight back at the entrance. "How are we going to get back out?"

"Plan was sleep here, leave at dawn," Karaya responded. "But plan change. Help me find source of wind." She held her hands out, indicating where she felt moving air.

Eddie stepped into the spot and felt a slight but steady stream of air on his right shoulder.

"Never feel before," said his companion. "Something open."

They both looked up. Eddie lifted the torch as far up as he could, but the cove ceiling was about twenty feet high. They could not see any visible opening.

"Logs," said Karaya. "From shipwreck. We climb."

Eddie understood what she meant. There weren't enough beams to stack, but they could prop some at low angles among the irregular rock arches to build a sort of slanting stairway. Within a few minutes, they had managed to place enough of them to rise a good twelve feet closer to the ceiling.

Standing on the top plank and holding the torch up, Karaya felt the air more strongly. "There," she pointed. "Small hole."

Eddie grabbed a log to wield, took Karaya's place atop the framework, and rammed the log against the hole. Debris crumbled down around them.

"Stand back," he alerted Karaya. Eddie had to stretch out as far as he could to punch against the ceiling, gripping the log as low as possible while still managing to give it some force. Part of the log broke off—it was too short to use at that point. Karaya found him another. After about fifteen minutes, he had widened the hole enough for them to squeeze through.

It was awkward anatomically, but there was no way around it: Karaya had to climb up onto Eddie, who assumed all her weight through her feet placed in his hands. He pushed her up as far as he could, she grabbed the rim of the hole, and at that moment, the beam they were standing on broke. Eddie tumbled to the ground and Karaya was left hanging by her hands, her legs and her long braid swiveling wildly.

She did not yell, but rather concentrated all her energy on pulling herself up. It was an enormous strain. Finding a purchase for her right foot against the rock wall, she pushed enough of her torso over the edge to hoist herself completely out. She disappeared from Eddie's sight for a moment, but then he saw her face appear over the hole. "Wait," she said.

It was a long wait. Eddie had plenty of time to ponder the bizarre events of his life over the past few months, and how completely the trappings of his previous life in England had fallen away—quite literally down to the shirt off his back. He sat down to wait, felt the sand against his bottom, and thought about how normal such a sensation against his bare skin had become. The life he was leading now was one he never could have predicted, and he had come close to losing it out there in the dark cove. But even as the torch was going out, Eddie's faith in Karaya held fast. He had not abandoned her. She would not abandon him.

Over an hour later, she reappeared, dangling the end of a rope from the hole they had opened in the cove ceiling. She had found her way back to the boat, retrieved the rope, and used a boulder to help her anchor one end of it. With her help, Eddie was able to pull himself out of the cove, instantly feeling the wet breeze from the sea all over his body as he surfaced into the night air. Then they moved the boulder on top of the hole to block the entrance.

There was no moonlight, but they were able to make their way down from the roof of the cove and around to where their boat was still moored. Eddie's arms and back and legs felt tired and sore. He could tell from their pace that Karaya was tired as well, but they needed to row the two miles back across the strait to the community.

They hadn't gone very far when Eddie, who was in the back of the rowboat, heard a faint splash behind them. Turning to look, he could barely make out that they were being followed by a canoe with a single rower. The hair on the back of his neck bristled. Without any need for scrutiny, he knew it was Hamid. Calmly he informed Karaya, who did not turn around to look. As quietly as possible, she let him know she had a plan.

As they approached the Jamaican shore, Karaya led them into a small inlet she knew on the way to where the *Ogba* lay at anchor, not yet visible. She and Eddie quickly fastened their rowboat to a mangrove root, took their oars, and hid close by, each in a different location. It was all Eddie could do to control his breathing.

Soon enough, Hamid edged his canoe into the little cove. Karaya did not even let him get completely out of the canoe before she rushed into the shallows with a great shout, smacking him over the head with her oar. He fell into the water, unconscious. Eddie and Karaya heaved him into a sitting position so Eddie could tie him up, but first Eddie removed Hamid's shirt—the only clothes he wore—revealing his emaciated chest.

"He's still famished," Eddie said.

"Then he will be willing to talk for food," was Karaya's conclusion.

Once they had bound Hamid using his mooring line, and had him gagged and blindfolded with strips torn from his shirt, Eddie undid Susanna's locket from Hamid's neck and hung it around his own. The thief had crudely latched the chain together after the clasp broke when he yanked it from Eddie's neck. Eddie saw the knife Hamid had stolen from him under the seat, and promptly placed it right back in the belted sheath he still wore. Then he laid Hamid out in the canoe he had been using, which Eddie now manned, and followed Karaya out of the inlet.

"I recognize this canoe," Eddie called over the water. "He took it from the mermaids."

Karaya nodded in response.

By the time they made it back to the *Ogba,* Hamid was stirring. Karaya and Eddie secured both boats, temporarily removed Hamid's blindfold, and marched him up the hill to the community. They replaced his blindfold just before nearing the gate. Karaya awakened Oshuna who, after receiving a full report from Eddie on what was known of Hamid's aggressions, ordered the man tied to the pole in the center of the circle. Then she ordered jerky, casabe bread and water for him.

"You have information. In our community we are as humane as we can be. If you behave, and share what you know, we'll see about untying you," Oshuna told Hamid, even though Eddie strongly advised against setting him loose.

"I don't know how he found us at the cove," Eddie said. "Does anyone else share the secret of its location?"

Oshuna looked at Karaya. They both shook their heads.

"The mermaids do not know," Oshuna said. "No one else. Not even Yewande knows where to find it."

"He stole a canoe from the mermaids, and somehow he followed us," Eddie said, his thoughts turning to Bronwen. He could imagine Hamid assaulting her, holding her at knifepoint with Eddie's own knife, demanding she tell him how to find the Sea Witch… but Bronwen could not have known about the cove. What could have led him there?

"Get some rest," ordered Oshuna. "I will question this man at dawn and explain to him very clearly what shall be the consequences should he fail to cooperate."

Chapter 13
Catch and Release

Yewande had gone looking for Eddie. "Come with me down to the *Ogba*," she told him. "I need to get some coriander and check on the yams."

Eddie knew the garden was important to her, but he also knew it was an opportunity for the two of them to be alone together. They had been enjoying each other's company more fondly with every passing day, and they had already exchanged a few furtive kisses and embraces. They set out, winding their way downhill through the tropical vegetation. Eddie would very much have liked to hold Yewande's hand as they walked, but this was no stroll through the English countryside. The relentless plant growth, and the community's understandable resistance to marking an easy path, made for a single-file progression, with Yewande in front.

Mesmerized for some while by Yewande's swiveling hips, Eddie tapped her shoulder. She turned, he drew her to him, and they embraced. Eddie whispered words of desire in her ear, and she laughed out loud.

"Eddie, love—you've made my skin pucker all over! Just look!'

He gladly confirmed this by admiring the taut skin on her breasts.

"But let me see under here…"

"Ooooh! That tickles!" Yewande shouted in a laughing fit.

Lost in their guffaws, they only gradually became aware of another noise.

"Hallo!? Help!"

The lovers grew silent and turned toward the source of the cries, where they met the gaze of someone trapped in the sprung net, hanging some fifteen feet above the ground.

"Eddie? Is that you?"

Eddie's body flushed hot and cold at the same time. "Bronwen?"

"I'm so embarrassed, Eddie. If you only knew everything I've been through to get here, only to step into a trap!"

"We'll get you down," said Yewande, moving to find the guide rope.

Eddie, glad to see her, tried to make light of the situation. "We've trapped a mermaid!"

"Very funny. It's not all that comfortable up here, you know, with my legs against my chest and my feet up over my head! Hmmm… I see you've recovered your locket."

"Yes! It's a long story… You, uh… how long have you been up there?" Eddie wanted to know.

"Hours," replied Bronwen. "Yes, Eddie, obviously I heard and saw everything you two just did. Traipsing through the jungle like Adam and Eve fresh from the apple."

"I can explain…" Eddie began, looking up at her pleadingly.

"Just help me down please. And stop gawking up my fanny!"

Neither Eddie nor Yewande had even thought to look up at her awkwardly exposed parts, but once Bronwen said that, they both took a good glance. Then Eddie helped Yewande undo the guide rope, lowering Bronwen gently to the ground. Together, they unloosed the top knot, and the net splayed out around her.

She stood up, approached Eddie, and embraced him. Then she introduced herself to Yewande. "Thank you both for rescuing me."

Eddie wore a look of frank admiration. "How did you get here?"

"Why the surprise? I told you I would come for you."

"I'm not surprised," said Eddie, furrowing his brow. "Just… curious."

"It's a long story," Bronwen said drily while darting her eyes toward his locket.

Yewande was watching the two of them and seized her moment to interject. "A long story, which Bronwen is going to tell me as she and I walk down together to the ship, where I'll treat her to some fresh guavas. Could you reset the trap, Eddie? Please?"

Eddie, still struggling to register Bronwen's arrival, could only nod.

"And then please go tell Oshuna that Bronwen has arrived."

In a matter of moments, the two women had disappeared downhill together, chatting like lifelong friends, their voices gradually lost to the distance. Eddie sighed heavily, bearing the clash of mixed emotions that rocked his heart like a storm-tossed ship. He focused on resetting the trap, with all its appropriate knots and its camouflage cover, and then returned to the community. When he dutifully told Oshuna of Bronwen's arrival, she raised one eyebrow but went right on spooning sunskin into little clay pots.

There didn't seem to be much that needed to be done with any urgency, and Waniyo was out with a hunting group, so Eddie sat down in the circle and was soon surrounded by children. Laurent, as Eddie discovered that afternoon, loved to listen to new words. Eddie would say a word in English, like *sky* as he pointed upward to indicate what it meant, and

Laurent would laugh uproariously, repeating the word and insisting that the correct term was *ciel*. This went on for some time, with Eddie's abdomen beginning to ache from so much laughing with the children. Then the children begged him to play hide-and-seek, and he always had to be the one to sit in the circle and count to thirty, practicing his French, before going to look for them.

"*…dix-huit, dix-neuf, vingt, vingt et un,…*"

When Eddie opened his eyes after counting through for the sixth round, he saw Yewande and Bronwen standing before him, delighted by his surprise. His unexpecting eyes suddenly took in their contrasts: Bronwen's body drew down toward the earth—her wide hips, so close to the ground, that framed her downward-facing mound, and her hefty breasts that hung low. Her long straight hair seemed to yearn for the earth. Yewande's taller and darker body, in contrast, sought the sky, with her puffy, frizzy hair, high hips and breasts and more forward-facing vulva.

Suddenly aware of his thoughts going astray, he blushed and looked down. "Good to see you both! Did you, uh… have a good walk together?"

The two women exchanged glances. "Yes," Bronwen replied. Then she smiled, and her eyes grew wide. "And, Yewande told me about the popcorn."

Eddie smiled, remembering Yewande's remark about many loves. He felt a tad uneasy, with both women standing there before him, and yet he also felt their support.
"Well, so, uh… What did you decide?"

Yewande raised an eyebrow. "Decide? About what?"

"About me."

The two women looked at each other and laughed.

"We didn't talk all that much about you, Eddie," said Bronwen. "You get to decide about you."

Yewande nodded. "What we decided together is that we like each other and want to get to know each other better."

Eddie looked from one to the other. "Can we, all three, like each other and get to know each other better? No hard feelings?"

"Yes," said Bronwen.

"Yes," said Yewande, who held out a hand to each of them. They stood for a long moment in a union of three wills.

"Also," Bronwen finally interrupted, "Now that we're all together, I need to tell you both about how I managed to get here."

As Bronwen began the story, Eddie was struck by how much of it he had already guessed. Yes, of course Hamid had waited until after Eddie had left the island, and then Bronwen had come back from fishing one afternoon only to find that Hamid had invaded the burrow—and of course, standing in front of Yewande, she was narrating the lurid details while using their mermaid names—"the Queen was tied up in her own hammock, and that bastard was wearing one of the Queen's blouses while holding the Empress with Eddie's knife to her throat!" As Eddie had predicted, Hamid had demanded not to be told how to find the Sea Witch, but rather that Bronwen escort him, "and I had never seen the Empress so distraught! Even though at the same time I couldn't help but remember how much she had championed that awful man over Eddie." Of course Bronwen had agreed, with an ulterior motive—"I knew it was a chance to come for you, Eddie"—and they set out that same afternoon in the canoe. Of course Hamid had attempted to have his way with Bronwen at some point, "but I knew we were close enough that I could swim if needed, so I simply kicked him and then bailed out of the boat. Oh he was furious!" Of course Bronwen had not wanted to lead him any further, so she swam, at great physical exertion, toward a different island, not knowing it was the island of the cove—"I hid in some brush close to the shore, until I saw him row by, and then I waited still some more before swimming here."

"Only to get caught in one of our traps," added Yewande. "Thankfully, it was the net and not the pit."

"It all makes sense," Eddie said, before relaying to Bronwen how he and Karaya had ambushed Hamid and escorted him to the community, where he was now captive. Realizing that Bronwen did not know about the cove, he told the story without revealing why he and Karaya had visited that island.

"Oh but please believe me, Eddie. I had no idea I was leading him toward you!"

"I believe you. How would you have known that Karaya and I were over there… gathering herbs?"

"Where's Hamid now?" Bronwen wanted to know.

"In one of the huts," said Eddie. "He wouldn't answer Oshuna's questions, so she had him bound, gagged, blindfolded and placed on low rations."

"Which hut?" Browen started to look around.

A screech and a brightly colored flash interrupted their conversation. "Barlo," squawked Onesimus. "Barlo!"

Yewande moved quickly, darting through the community circle to find her mother.

"Yes, I heard," Oshuna said to her daughter. "And I knew that this day would come sooner or later. Please stow all the materials."

Yewande stared at her. "Are you going to let him in?"

"That," Oshuna said with a shake of her shoulders, "depends on whether he comes in peace."

Karaya took Yewande's hand and they went to hide the sunskin ingredients.

"Higgins, Eddie," Oshuna called. "Go meet Barlo and escort him and his crew back up here. We don't need any of them in the traps today. I think I know why they've come, but see if you can get a sense of their purpose."

By the time the two Englishmen encountered them, the skinners had made it about halfway up the hill. Antonio had skillfully led them around the pit. They were glad to see Eddie and embraced him one and all with some good-natured ribbing, except Barlo, who merely patted his shoulder. Eddie introduced them to Higgins.

James Clayton looked Eddie over, up and down. "Why didn't you stay with the mermaids, mate?"

Eddie and Higgins stole a look. "The mermaids work with the Sea Witch," Eddie replied. "They have a… mutual understanding."

"A mermaid that walks and a bird that talks," muttered Mr. Ola.

"She be a powerful witch," muttered Raintree, and Eddie noticed his hands shook as he spoke.

Higgins led the way back up the hill, around the net, and soon they arrived at the community, where their presence was announced with a blast on the conch shell. There was a brief pause in which not even Eddie or Higgins knew what to expect, before Oshuna herself appeared over the top of the wall. Eddie knew she stood on the defense ledge that had been built along the high back of the wall.

"Captain Barlo and crew," she announced. "To what do we owe the pleasure?"

Barlo puffed out his chest. "We've come for the gold."

Oshuna laughed, loud and clear and long. Then, suddenly furious, she asked, "The gold?"

"Yes, Oshuna," Barlo replied. "The gold you owe me, as we agreed in Cartagena. You told me about the zemi, remember?"

"The agreement," she interrupted him, "is null and void. You were to keep Mr. Fife as your crew member, and yet within days you had bartered him off to the mermaids."

"There was no stipulation as to the length of time that he would serve on my crew!"

"You would have killed him and my dear Higgins too, had I not stopped you! The point is, captain, you are not a man of your word."

"Ah, how you still sting," Barlo said, his nostrils flaring. "Your dear Higgins, is it?" With a nod toward Eddie's former first mate, Barlo ordered Jabari to detain him. In an instant, Higgins felt Jabari's sword across his throat.

Oshuna fixed Barlo in her steely gaze. "Release him immediately," she intoned. "My guards have arrows and stones trained on you and your men at this very instant. You are outnumbered."

Barlo slowly forced a smile. "Very well," he said. "Let us enter in peace. I request parley."

Oshuna waited a long moment before answering. "Your request is granted, provided you lay down all your weapons at the gate. And captain…"

"More conditions?" he interrupted.

"Release. My. Dear. Higgins."

"Ah yes," said Barlo, and at his sign, Jabari freed his captive, who rubbed some blood from his neck before turning right around to relieve Jabari of his sword.

Eddie and Higgins collected the weapons that Barlo and his crew abandoned and left them with the gate guards. The men were led inside. This time, there was neither drumming nor dancing to meet the newcomers, only looks of hostility and suspicion. Jabari furrowed his brow and squinted his eyes when he saw Bronwen, unable to remember where he had seen her before.

"This will not be a private parley," Oshuna announced. "We will hold it right here in the community circle, and any who wish to attend are welcome."

"I find this… acceptable," replied Barlo with thinly disguised disappointment.

"And we will begin the parley," Oshuna continued, "with your account of how you found our community."

There were jeers and shouts from among the dozen or so people who had assembled. Barlo looked around him, assessing the scene, and detained his gaze on Bronwen. "I see there is one among us," the captain began, "who has abandoned her fins for legs. I should have suspected as much. Let us see if she will contradict my version of the events. When my crew and I summoned the mermaids and presented our barter, this one here you see before us now, she spurned our offer. There was another mermaid with her in the water, but there must have been a third on land who, with accomplished devilry, caused the sun to burn our sails. In the confusion, we had a captive on board who provoked a skirmish, and we lost both the captive and Mr. Fife to the sea. The mermaids," and here he pointed at Bronwen, "did not fulfill their agreement for the barter. So we repaired our sails and swung back out to open waters, just far enough away for our look-out to do his job. Clayton and Antonio took turns on watch for several days, until we saw you arrive in the *Ogba*. We followed you at great distance, but we also awaited information from the captive who had fallen into the sea with Fife."

Oshuna raised an eyebrow. "The one called Hamid?"

Barlo nodded. "He was to relay to me what knowledge he could find about your supply of gold. In the end he betrayed us, but we were still able to follow his rowboat, with this mermaid he had with him until she jumped ship."

Oshuna raised her other eyebrow. "Where is the *Capricorn*?"

"She rests in the same inlet as the *Ogba*," Barlo replied.

Oshuna dropped her head into her hands and spoke from that position. "Unlike you, Captain Barlo, I have dedicated time and resources to helping people escape from slavery. Many of them live right here and are present with us now. Quite a few of them brave the sea with me in our search to help others escape. We all have a great need for our community to be hidden, to be protected, and we have successfully evaded the British authorities, and the Spaniards before them, here on Jamaica for twenty years now." She lifted her head to glare at Barlo. "That inlet can barely hide my ship, much less both of ours together. You have drawn undue attention to our whereabouts."

Barlo looked to his men and nodded at Mr. Ola. "I agree. We can leave very quickly, just as soon as you give me the gold."

"I gave you what I owed you in Cartagena," she replied, "or have you already forgotten?"

Barlo forced an exaggerated smile. "We agreed—or perhaps you have forgotten?—that what you gave me in Cartagena was insufficient."

"But you broke the terms of our agreement when you bartered Eddie to the mermaids! We have been around this ring before."

Oshuna's face registered annoyance, then alarm, then resignation as her macaw's piercing squawks demanded everyone's attention yet again.

"Enemy alert!" repeated Onesimus as he flew around the circle.

A guard, panting from his sprint up the hill, confirmed that a third ship had weighed anchor just outside the inlet, and a group of men were exploring the area.

"Slave catchers," Yewande said. "It is only a matter of time before they find us."

Oshuna nodded. "This is your moment of truth, Captain Barlo," she scoffed. "Directly or indirectly, you led the slave catchers here. Will you and your men fight to defend us?"

Barlo's gaze hardened. He spat on the ground. Without breaking eye contact with Oshuna, he pointed at Yewande and uttered a word in Yoruba.

Oshuna's calm expression broke. "No!"

Mr. Ola, the only other person who had understood his captain's command, grabbed Yewande and held her with his knife to her throat.

"Where," Barlo repeated, "is the gold?"

Tears streamed down Oshuna's face. "Behold your treasure, Tokunbo," she sobbed. "Yewande is your daughter."

Mr. Ola flinched, his knife wavering.

Barlo stood, unmoving but not unmoved. He appeared as a man determined to detain a flood with only the look in his eyes, until it inevitably overtook him, cascading down his cheeks. Mr. Ola, Sijuwola, released the daughter of his old friend Tokunbo, and Eddie and Bronwen ran to her.

Oshuna stepped in to embrace the father of her child, and instantly she was all that kept him from collapsing to the ground. "Help us," she said. "We have so little time."

She released him, but he just stared at her blankly. "Save your daughter," she added. "Help save us all."

He made no reply but moved quickly to Yewande and bowed before her. "Please forgive me, daughter. I did not know."

She bowed with him, her tears falling to the ground. "I forgive you, father. I did not know either."

They pulled themselves up into an embrace. There followed some rushed words between mother, father, and daughter in Yoruba. All were crying. Eddie and the others present could only stare in wonder.

Chapter 14
Warpaint

Oshuna interrupted the family reunion with a sad smile. "Well, captain, we have attackers on the way. Will you defend your daughter, and the rest of us as well?"

"I will," he replied resolutely.

Oshuna nodded and glanced at Marie. "We can guess why the slave catchers are coming."

"*Pardon!*" cried Marie. "*Je suis désolée.*"

"How many?" interjected Barlo.

"I saw six," replied the guard.

"They are outnumbered," observed Oshuna. "Even without your crew."

"And they may lose some of their number to the traps," added Yewande.

Barlo nodded. "But they are most likely armed."

Oshuna took a deep breath. "Tokunbo of Owo, after all these years you have finally come here to my community. You have seen how I have designed and developed it to be self-sufficient. Do you think the wall and a pair of traps are our only defenses?"

She turned to Waniyo. "Quickly. You know the protocol. Eddie, go with him and help as you can."

As the witnesses of the parley rushed to their bohios, Waniyo directed Eddie to silently appear in the doorways of the various homes while making a large "X" with his forearms. At the first home, an elderly woman saw him, nodded gravely, and leapt into action, searching among her possessions. There were similar responses in the other homes, until Eddie inadvertently found the hut where Hamid was still bound, gagged and blindfolded. Eddie almost felt sorry for him as he simply moved on to the next bohio.

The circle filled with the community members as they emptied their homes. They piled up their items in the circle: drums, buckets, ropes, arrows, spears and lances. Waniyo revived the fire, and several women tossed palm-size stones into the flames. Other women were quickly painting designs on the bodies of the warriors. Most of the men, including Eddie, Higgins, Barlo and his crew—and Yewande, Bronwen, Karaya and a few more women—soon wore skeletal white stripes branching out along their ribs from a central white trunk that stretched from sternum to genitals, with white circles around the eyes and mouth and a white stripe down the nose. Some had white swirls around their thighs as well, but there wasn't time for anything more elaborate.

Everyone worked in silence. Buckets full of hot rocks were passed to warriors who mounted the defense ledge behind the wall. The ropes, drums, and weapons were distributed. Barlo's men drew their knives, except Jabari, who gave his sword to Higgins again, with a shrug, and then claimed the longest lance to heat its tip in the fire.

Oshuna appeared among them, seeming to float in a glimmering gossamer gown of gold. Eddie remembered this robe from the first time he had seen her on the wharf in Cartagena. Barlo obviously remembered it, too. Her radiance drew the attention of her former lover, at first indirectly, and then in frank admiration.

The warriors stood at the ready, just inside the gate. Oshuna stood behind them, in the circle, holding a conch shell, and as she drew it close to her lips, Eddie followed her gaze to the portcullis. One of the community guards, on one side, and James Clayton, on the other, were spying through cracks in the wall. The guard turned and nodded to

Oshuna—the invaders were arriving. She mouthed the words "How many?" and James Clayton held up six fingers.

"They evaded the traps," whispered Bronwen.

"Or they rescued each other, like we rescued you," whispered Yewande.

"MMWAAAAAAAAANGH" mourned the conch shell from Oshuna's mouth. Once again, the air exploded in reverberations, as Waniyo and five other drummers pounded a furious cadence. Barlo roared, Antonio howled, Yewande ululated, Jabari moaned, and in the general commotion Eddie hoped sincerely that the slave catchers felt fear deep in their bones.

A single shot rang out, but the noise from the community did not cease. Only after another few rounds had been fired into the air did Oshuna signal sudden silence.

"No need for hostilities," came a voice from beyond the wall. "We're here for the boy! Turn him over and we'll be on our way."

"What… boy…?" growled Barlo.

"Son of a slave woman goes by Marie. Bounty on her head, too, but we jes' want the boy."

"Tell us why you want him," yelled Oshuna.

"Well he ain't no good to you, now, is he? Only about three years old, maybe four," said a second voice.

"Exactly," Oshuna replied. "So he isn't any good to you either."

"That boy," replied the first voice with a cough and a spit, "will allow us to live real comfortable for a while."

Barlo stared at Oshuna, then winked. "We'll kill the boy, then, and throw the body to you over the wall."

Everyone in the community knew this was a bluff.

"No need for anybody to get kilt," came the first voice again.

"Besides, he ain't worth no bounty to us iffen he's dead," said the second voice.

"What is so special about him?" asked Oshuna. "Why is he worth all this risk?"

There was no answer for a long while. Jabari began shaking his head and stretching his arms, itching to launch his lance over the gate.

Finally there came a familiar cough. "We can offer you a part of the bounty."

"You take us for fools!" shouted Barlo.

Oshuna moved to Barlo's side and placed her hand on his shoulder. "We have no interest in coin. Our interest is to know why you want the boy."

"Well he's the plantation owner's son, inne? He wants him, he does," said the second voice. "Taylor Hemsworth wants his son, his property."

The slave catcher's words hung in the air like a poison that Eddie fought to avoid inhaling. His heart sank to his gut while his blood rose to his ears. How could this be? Susanna's father, the man he had thought might one day be his father-in-law, was the man who had raped Marie…? Her son, Laurent, was no one's property… he was Susanna's half-brother, a brother she surely did not even know she had...

Eddie clutched his hand to his locket, his face contorted and flushed. "Never!"

His shout was so sudden, so unexpected, that it triggered Jabari, who sent his lance soaring over the wall. All was suspended during the terrible moments in which the weapon could not be recalled… until the silence was pierced by a cry of pain from beyond the wall, then a short burst of bullets.

"Take cover," shouted Oshuna, even as many of the community members were already fleeing the gate area.

James Clayton, Antonio, Bronwen and the guards held their positions on the defense ledge below the top of the wall, peeking over to launch hot rocks at the aggressors.

Eddie saw James Clayton aim a steaming stone straight down beyond the wall. Rather than throw the stone, he let it fall, then turned around with a gleeful look on his face as he ducked back down on the ledge. "Clothes!" he yelled, with a wink at Eddie. "A definite disadvantage." Then he held up his fist, raising one finger per second. At the third finger came a shriek.

"My arse!" bellowed a slave catcher.

"Yer breeches are on fire!" yelled another.

"You're better off without 'em, mate," called James Clayton. They heard the man whooping as he struggled to pull off his pants, and they all allowed themselves a moment of mirth.

But it was short-lived.

"Now!" came a voice from outside the wall. Soon there was a terrible hissing noise that grew louder overhead as a bomb landed just inside the gate. The bomb wasn't held together very well, already spurting pebbles into the leaking smoke.

A second bomb with a longer trajectory landed somewhere among the homes nearest the circle.

"Run!" yelled Barlo.

The first explosion blew open the gate. Mr. Ola, limping away as quickly as he could, was hit by a barrage of pebbles that knocked him over. He covered his head as he lay on the ground.

The second bomb exploded on the roof of one of the bohios, setting it ablaze. The stinking smoke was still clearing as Eddie counted all six slave catchers streaming through the entrance, some of them shooting indiscriminately into the haze. The last two stopped just inside the gate, and Eddie couldn't understand why until he saw that Oscar had confronted them. The coati stood on his hind legs, chattering and nattering at them, wriggling his snout all around like only a coati can, and he detained the surprised men just long enough that Antonio and James Clayton, still on the defense ledge above and behind the slave catchers, were able to jump together onto their backs. The invaders staggered but remained upright, so the two skinners, with their legs around the men's waists, steered them toward each other, each punching the other's man in the face, before finally knocking their heads together and jumping off their backs.

Eddie, Yewande and Waniyo ran forward to meet the invaders. "That one's mine!" yelled Yewande fiercely as she launched to the lead, stopping abruptly to ground her stance right in front of a clothed man rushing toward her. Giving a great shout, she swung her staff with practiced force, connecting against the man's wrist and knocking the pistol from his grasp, sending it spinning into the heavy smoke. Quicker than thinking, she swung the other end of the staff around and struck his head, slamming him to the ground.

"For Amadi!" she yelled at the prone man as she smacked his skull again, definitively, with her staff.

Eddie caught her eye quickly. "Was he the one that killed…?"

She nodded. "I am not proud of killing, Eddie, but I act in the name of justice."

At the same moment, Waniyo swung his staff between the legs of another invader, tripping him. Eddie heard the man hit the ground, followed by the sound of a muffled explosion and a cry of agony. Blood seeped through the man's shirt; he had accidentally shot himself in the abdomen.

Yewande approached Eddie and yelled into his ear. "Where is Marie? Where is Laurent?"

Out of the smoke behind Yewande there suddenly loomed another slave catcher—it was the one who James Clayton had left pantsless. Eddie's mouth and eyes rounded as he raised his staff, ready to defend Yewande, but the man suddenly lurched toward her, almost reaching her before falling face down onto the ground. Protruding from his buttock was a small arrow. "It is one of Karaya's poison darts," said Yewande. They looked for Karaya but couldn't see her through the smoke and confusion.

Eddie grabbed Yewande's hand and they ran toward the burning bohio. Oshuna stood outside, directing community members toward the back wall of the palisade, where Higgins was leading them through the emergency tunnel exit. A few brave community members were putting out the fire with water from the rain barrels.

"This is where I had Hamid bound to the pole," Oshuna said when she saw her daughter with Eddie. "But the whole structure has collapsed. He's either dead or escaped."

"Where's Marie? And her children?" Yewande asked again.

"I don't know!" Oshuna wailed. "Please find them!"

Eddie began searching nearby. By the time he made it to the next bohio, he heard muffled yells. Three bohios away, he rushed in and found Marie tied to the central pole with Dominique at her chest. Eddie quickly removed her gag.

"That man… took Laurent," Marie cried. "*Secours!*"

Knife in hand, Eddie severed the rope quickly. "How long ago?"

"*Quelques minutes…*"

"Fopdoodle! Mumblecrust!" The vocabulary, punctuated by grunts, could only have been Bronwen's. Eddie rushed outside to find her launching insults at Hamid, who was running away while holding a kicking and screaming toddler on one hip. He was running with Laurent to the one slave catcher left standing.

"I couldn't bear to throw rocks at him," yelled Bronwen. "What if I hit the child?"

"Hamid!" Eddie called, his staff poised, Bronwen at his side. He knew, just as she had said, that he wouldn't be able to strike the man without also hitting the boy. "Why do you trust that slave catcher? You think he will give you any part of the bounty?"

Marie had followed Eddie, holding Dominique tight, and stood watching the scene. Mother and infant were both sobbing. Waniyo heard them and came running. Oshuna and Yewande approached, and then Antonio, James Clayton, and Jabari.

"And you," Eddie addressed the slave catcher. "The man holding your bounty has betrayed every single one of us standing here. You think he won't betray you as well?"

The bounty hunter eyed Hamid uneasily. "Gimme the boy," he said. "I'll split the pay-out. These people are our witne…"

The thump of a rock hitting his skull interrupted the man, who slumped to the ground with a huge gash bleeding along his cheek.

Mr. Ola limped out from behind a tree. "I hit him in the head, but I'll bet he isn't dead."

His victim moaned and clutched his jaw. Hamid took advantage of the confusion and began to sprint toward the gate, still carrying the boy. Eddie, Yewande, and Bronwen immediately chased him through the community circle.

Hamid stopped so suddenly that Eddie almost ran into him. There before them, framed by the ruined gateway, stood Barlo. He held a pistol aimed at Hamid's chest. Eddie recalled that a firearm had flown from the hand of one of the invaders when Yewande struck him.

"Put that boy down," ordered Barlo.

Hamid did not move. Neither did Laurent, suddenly terrified. Both of them had their eyes on the gun.

"I know where the gold is," said Hamid.

"That is no concern to me now," Barlo replied.

"You tell me!" Hamid insisted. "You tell me to find where she hide the gold. And I find. I did find."

"Is that so?" asked Oshuna, who had arrived and heard the exchange, as had most everyone else.

"Traitor!" roared Barlo. "A thousand times a traitor!"

Hamid shifted Laurent so that the boy blocked his chest and head. The boy began to kick and whine.

Barlo shook with rage. "You would use this child as a shield? Such cowardice I will not abide!" He cocked the pistol.

Before anyone could predict it, Hamid had thrown the boy straight toward the pistol, just as Barlo had changed his target to Hamid's foot. He squeezed the trigger… but there was no recoil. The pistol had no more ammunition.

Hamid turned to run but was surprised to see Marie standing right behind him. She gave him a sharp kick in the groin, and as he doubled over in pain, Eddie and Yewande were already beating him with their staffs.

After a few long moments in which those present were satisfied to see Hamid get beaten, and to see Laurent run to his mother's tight embrace with Waniyo holding Dominique at their side, Oshuna raised her arms. "Enough! Guards, bind the villain immediately!"

Two guards approached Barlo with a length of rope.

"Not him," Oshuna specified rather begrudgingly. She pointed to Hamid. "This one lying here."

"And there lies another with a broken jaw, over by the burnt bohio," said Yewande. "Bind him, too."

"And these others here near the gate," said Antonio, pointing to the two that he and his mate had jumped.

"Round up and detain any survivors," Oshuna ordered the guards.

"A question have I," spoke Barlo. "Where is Raintree?"

No one knew the answer.

"Are all accounted for?" asked Oshuna. "Higgins led most of the community through the tunnel around the backside of the slope to the beach. They were to go on around to the inlet, where they await my signal to return. But where is Karaya?"

"Here!" came a familiar voice. Oshuna followed it, moving quickly toward the rubble of the gate, with Barlo and Eddie at her side. There sat Karaya, pressing leaves onto the chest of Raintree, who lay across her lap.

"Gunfire," she said. "When they broke through the gate."

"By the stars," exclaimed Barlo. He leaned down and cupped the man's chin. "Raintree, mate, can you hear me?"

Karaya looked at Oshuna and shook her head. "Nothing I can do."

His eyes stinging, Barlo started to shake Raintree, whose glorious octopus tattoo, already partially covered by the white warpaint, had become a bloody pink mess.

Raintree opened his eyes. With ragged breaths, he managed to give his captain his final words. "I believe in mermaids. And witches. It was an honor to fight with them for justice... and freedom."

His jaw went slack as his eyes shut and his head rolled to the side.

Eddie knelt beside the man who had "birthed" him, befriended him and taught him the ropes aboard the

Capricorn. Mr. Ola and the rest of Barlo's crew hung their heads as James Clayton sang a plaintive dirge.

When he finished, Oshuna sounded a call on the conch shell. It was appropriately doleful, but it also signaled to the escaped community members that the conflict had ended.

Chapter 15
A New World

Two of the slave catchers had survived the assault, and their fates were yet to be determined, along with that of Hamid. Between Barlo, who wanted to execute them all, and Karaya, who wanted to heal them before sending them away, it was up to Oshuna to assert her authority over the gathered assemblage. Yewande, Eddie, Bronwen and Waniyo looked on.

"I appreciate your opinion, Tokunbo, but you are only a guest here. I'm more inclined to follow the advice of my wise physic, yet I feel, Karaya, that your solution is too generous. The problem is that even if I were to release the survivors immediately, without attention to their wounds, then they still might make it to a city or port and reveal the location of our community. Our security would be irrevocably compromised, especially that of Marie and her family. I will reach a decision soon, but in the meantime: Guards, relieve them of their clothes."

The two survivors were quickly stripped. Eddie noted their obvious relief from escaping a summary execution, but only one of them appeared to also feel relief from escaping his clothes. The other put up a lot of futile resistance.

Barlo ran his hands over his head, pacing in exasperation. "What about their ship?"

"The ship you are referring to," said Oshuna, "is now mine, since I had already instructed Higgins to occupy it with the community members who escaped with him."

Barlo sneered. "I see. So the ship is yours, you say. And who shall sail it?"

"If needed, Higgins can captain it."

"Hadn't you said that the inlet barely hides one ship, let alone two? Let me take it," Barlo pressed.

"I will not let you take it. I might, however, sell it to you," Oshuna added with a wink.

"Sell it to me?! You would not have defeated those slave catchers without me and my crew!"

"Who could say? It was your man, wasn't it—that big fellow—who threw his lance prematurely and started the whole conflagration!"

"You would have simply given them the boy?"

"Of course not! How dare you! As I told you, there are other defenses that…"

Oshuna and Barlo had been inching closer together during this dispute, until they each felt one of Yewande's palms on their chests.

"Mother of Pearl, F…ather… of Steel," she began, looking back and forth to each, "listen to me. As we have all just recently learned, I am the product of you both. I am one half of each of you, in a way. Therefore, I will take the ship, and if either of you need it or need my services, you can trust me to respond."

Oshuna smiled from ear to ear. "It's a wonderful plan, daughter. Thank you."

Barlo squinted at her but couldn't hide the grin playing on his cheeks. "You wish me to trust you to make decisions? Then answer, what would you have us do with Hamid? What is his punishment?"

Yewande set her arms akimbo and thought for a few moments. "That man seems irredeemable. He continues to act exclusively in his own interest and does not hesitate to throw others in harm's way."

"Quite precisely that, yes," agreed her mother.

"My determination is to ask you, father, to maroon him, along with the two slave catchers."

Barlo rubbed his chin, tugging at his beard. "For that I'll still have to hold them on board the *Capricorn*, and keep a watch, and feed them a bit, until such time as we can find a deserted little key somewhere to deposit them."

Yewande merely crossed her arms defiantly and stared at him.

"Wouldn't you rather," began her father, "tie that traitor to a boulder and drop him into the sea?"

Oshuna reached for Barlo's hand and drew his gaze to hers. "This is why I left you all those years ago. Tokunbo. Do not let your heart be ruled by rancor nor cruelty. The man deserves punishment, but there is no need for such an extreme."

"You understand that he will most likely die soon after we maroon him?" he countered. "All three of them."

"Yes," replied Oshuna. "But they may survive, and one way or another, they will have had a chance. If one of them survives and reveals our location, then so be it. We will have to be ready."

"Let it be their fate," added their daughter. "If you wish, we can supply the food you will need for them on the way."

"It is agreed, then," spoke Barlo, admiring his daughter's force of will. Oshuna still held his hand. He turned to her with an uneasy objectivity. "Why? Why did you hide her from me?"

Oshuna looked him in the eyes with a steady stare. "You had no love left in you. It was the reason I chose to keep your identity hidden from Yewande. Do you have any love in you now?"

"I…" Barlo looked uneasy, and giving up on words altogether, he attempted to kiss Oshuna.

She stepped back. "It is not that easy. I am not sure how I feel about you, or if I can come to trust you again."

Barlo tried and failed to hide his incredulity. "In spite of everything that has transpired in the defense of your community?"

Yewande dropped her arms from her chest. "This is a good moment for me to take my leave. You two captains may finish this conversation alone." She turned and walked right past Eddie and Bronwen.

"Where is she going?" asked Bronwen.

"She's heading to that tall ceiba," said Eddie as he watched her. "It's where she speaks to her husband's ghost."

As the sun set and the night creatures began their callings, three couples formed. Eddie with Bronwen in the circle, Oshuna with Barlo in her bohio, and Yewande with Amadi under the ceiba, explored rambling routes of the heart and mind in three intense and simultaneous conversations. Karaya in her hammock, Barlo's men sitting around the fire reminiscing about Raintree, Marie and Waniyo putting the children to bed with extra care on that night, Higgins and the others returning from the inlet, might have caught these fragments of dialogue shuffled on the breeze, without quite knowing who said what or at which moments: "I have always loved you," "I thought you abandoned me," "I missed you," "What do we do now?", "Will they return?", "I need you," and "Thank you for being here."

An hour later, when Yewande returned from the ceiba, she found Bronwen and Eddie still together. They stopped talking as she approached, and she sat in silence with them.

Eddie took her hand. "What did Amadi say?"

Yewande remained quiet for a few moments. "He thanked me for avenging him. And… he released me."

Bronwen furrowed her brow. "Released you?"

"Or he released himself," Yewande continued. "He told me he was leaving me in your hands, and he bid me farewell."

Yewande shed a few tears, choking a bit on these words. Eddie embraced her, even as he felt the need to ask her, "Whose hands? Mine, right?"

"Both of yours. All four hands. Six hands together," Yewande answered, pulling away from Eddie to grasp both their hands in hers. "He said he wasn't sure, but he thought my best future can be forged with both of you."

Bronwen giggled nervously. "He told you all that, did he?"

"But what does that mean?" Eddie urged.

Yewande squeezed their four hands and released them. "It means what we want it to mean. Look at us, living without clothes, nor king, nor priest—we do what we want to do. Eddie, you are the newest of us to living like this. Are you adapted to it?"

"Adapted and very comfortable, yes," Eddie replied. "I don't think I could ever go back to my old life."

Bronwen gave him a sideways glance. "Not even for Susanna?"

"We live such different lives now, she and I," Eddie said with a shrug. "I was thinking about how Laurent is her half-brother. Who would have imagined? But even if she somehow came here for him, I don't think I would want to be involved. Besides, it's better she doesn't know about Laurent, nor he about her, don't you think?"

"It is information that we can hold until such time as it may be important to release," said Yewande.

"Laurent is still in danger," added Bronwen. "We all are."

"Yes," said Yewande, "and there is a ship waiting for me in the inlet, which I haven't even seen yet, but that I can use to transport Marie and her family somewhere else, should she choose. Or to bring reinforcements here."

Eddie stood and faced Yewande, touching his brow. "Aye, cap'n!"

"Oh yes, Mr. Fife?" Yewande addressed him with uncharacteristic formality. "You would sail with me?"

"I'd follow you anywhere, captain."

Yewande turned to Bronwen. "And you, Princess?"

She blushed. "I miss my siren sisters, but I don't need to go by Princess anymore. Especially not under your orders, captain."

Yewande smiled. Once again she took their hands, and this time she led them under the branches of the ceiba. Eddie opened his mouth to ask what they were doing, but she covered it with a kiss. Then she kissed Bronwen while pulling Eddie closer to her. Soon their three bodies moved as one, in a special bliss none of them had known before.

***

Raintree's funeral was held at dawn. There was a far corner within the community palisade that served as a cemetery, and Barlo and his crew had excavated a tomb and placed some stones together as a marking. The four perished slave catchers had already been buried in a mass grave outside the community's walls.

"Wallace Raintree was a trusted advisor, a skilled cook, and most of all, a good friend," spoke Barlo. "May he rest in peace."

Mr. Ola cleared his throat. "May the spirit of our steadfast friend live on, through us, to speak again."

Marie stepped forward, holding Laurent's hand. "*J'honore votre sacrifice en défendant mon fils*," she said, and Yewande translated for all to hear: "I honor your sacrifice in defending my son."

"As do we all," Oshuna added. "All of us honor the sacrifice of those who defend our community."
James Clayton sang a brief hymn, and it was over.

Yewande took Eddie's hand. "I will plant some roses here."

"That would be good, yes," Eddie mused. "They're a symbol of England. He denounced his homeland with fervor, but it was a fervor that could only have been born from a true son of Britain."

***

Barlo inspected the escape tunnel and determined that it would be an easier route for getting his prisoners aboard the *Capricorn*. He confirmed with Oshuna that there were no shoals or hidden reefs near the open beach on that side of the community, in which case it was merely a matter of moving his ship from the inlet around the peninsula to the beach.

"Father," began Yewande, "stay long enough to attend my wedding."

"Of course, dear one. Who are you marrying?"

"Eddie and Bronwen. They don't know it yet."

"What riddle is this?"

"No riddle," Oshuna interjected. "It's a splendid idea."

"Three… together?" stuttered Barlo.

"Oh, come now, Tokunbo," Oshuna responded. "Aren't you the one always going on about how we live in the New World, where the rules of the Old World no longer apply? You've been saying that for decades. Well then, we are free to create new bonds however we see fit."

Barlo nodded. "I suppose that's true."

"You," Oshuna said with a wink, "are just jealous. Perhaps it's time for you to settle down somewhere and forge the bond, or bonds, you desire."

Barlo had no reply.

Eddie and Bronwen, in contrast, had two kinds of replies: both gave an immediate and enthusiastic yes to Yewande's proposal under the ceiba, and then a much, much longer response that entailed an intricate choreography among the three of them as to how, exactly, a union of three could work. Questions as to which of them would be responsible for what, the desire for children, where they would live, and how their wedding ceremony would take place were all addressed. Often, to Eddie's surprise, he found himself more hesitant on certain aspects of their potential union than the two women, who mostly presented a united front. Flustered, he remembered he was the newest of the three of them to the New World, and thus the one who still felt the old societal norms and pressures the most keenly.

Yewande placed her palm on the back of his hand and gently twisted. "Remember, Eddie? Sometimes it takes two to free a stubborn third."

He smiled, recalling the very large oyster that he and Yewande had loosed together, and then he agreed, he agreed, he agreed to everything, coming to an understanding that his happiness would more likely spring all the more forthrightly if the two of them—Bronwen and Yewande—were already of the same mind on so many matters.

And so it happened that the wedding followed the funeral, one day after the other, but the wedding was to take place an hour or so before dusk, after every able-bodied person, including Barlo and his men, had spent the time between the one ceremony and the other helping to repair the gate and the burnt-out bohio, and keeping watch over the three boats in the inlet. The wedding was to take place on the beach that was downhill from the community on the side of the escape tunnel. Barlo, keen to rid himself of the prisoners already cooped up in his brig, moved the *Capricorn* from the inlet to the beach so that he and his crew could embark after the ceremony.

Anticipating his new life with Yewande and Bronwen, Eddie no longer wanted to wear the locket. He judged it to be a good gift for Laurent and found a moment to give it to him. He told the boy, in halting French, that Susanna was a special friend who lived faraway, and that maybe he would meet her someday. Marie, who knew the truth, felt uncomfortable with the gift, but she knew her son had not really understood what Eddie had told him. She saw that the chain would break again soon and guessed that her son would easily forget the entire situation.

It was a quickly designed wedding, but not for that any less beautiful. All the community, and Barlo and his crew, stood in a circle, and no one wore anything, of course, except for the flowers in the hair of the three spouses. Each spouse lit a tallow candle from the same flame, on a candle held by Oshuna, and then each used their candle to burn through a separate spot on a long, sturdy vine that Karaya held for them. The vine was left in four pieces. The candles were extinguished and set aside. Then each of them picked up two sections of the vine and knotted them together—first Bronwen, then Eddie, then Yewande. Oshuna took the reconstituted vine and bound together their six hands with it, chanting in Yoruba. Then she asked each of them in turn to bear witness to the kiss between the other two, before the three of them leaned forward into a common kiss over their bound hands.

Oshuna gave vows for each to repeat, one after the other over the sound of the gentle waves: "My love I give to each of you and to both of you, so that there may be more love in the world. Let us live and love together, for this is the desire of our hearts."

190

Then Oshuna raised her right hand and asked for all assembled to do the same. "We bear witness," she said, "to the union of Eddie, and Bronwen, and Yewande, the three of them together, and welcome their union in our community."

While the community cheered in affirmative response, Oshuna informed the spouses they would need to work together to unbind themselves. It was a clever trick, because the binding was more thorough than any of them had realized. The three spouses were forced to raise their arms over their heads and bend over backwards and forwards, and weave in and out between each other's arms, pressing themselves against each other in oddly intimate positions, all to the great amusement of the community.

When they finished, the trio stood for a moment hand in hand in hand, their eyes glistening, marveling at the strength of their shared love.

This was the deep reverie they were immensely enjoying when suddenly a flash against the setting sun caught Eddie's eye. It was the glint from a sword… in the hands of Hamid. In a heartbeat, Eddie had unsheathed his knife from his belt that lay nearby and rushed forward to attack.

"My sword!" yelled Barlo. "And my turban!"

"Eddie, no!" came the shouts from all around.

The traitor had somehow escaped, filched Barlo's items, and made it ashore, evidently to slip away unnoticed or attack anyone who got in the way of his freedom. In a moment of wild inspiration, Eddie rushed him from the side, calling out to startle him as he slid toward Hamid's legs, knife at the ready. Hamid leapt into the air, sword high, and Eddie used his knife in a way he had never done before: to harm someone… He stabbed Hamid in the sole of his foot, in one swift motion pulling the knife back flat against his chest and rolling out of reach along the surf.

Hamid crumpled to the sand, groaning in pain and shouting curses in his language. He quickly stood and took a few hops toward Eddie, waving his sword, but Eddie kicked the leg he stood on. As he fell, Hamid swung the sword and it nicked Eddie's shin, but Eddie was still able to jump on him, pin his arms, and subdue him face down on the beach. They were quickly surrounded by many of the onlookers including Barlo, Higgins, Oshuna's guards, and Eddie's two newly betrothed.

"Enough!" Barlo roared, clearing everyone away and snatching back his sword and turban. He rolled Hamid over, placed his foot heavily on his chest, and pressed the point of his sword against the fallen man's neck. "I should kill you now and be done with it!"

"Aye, cap'n!" yelled James Clayton, who'd quickly boarded the *Capricorn* to see how many had escaped. "He's killed the other two prisoners!"

Barlo pressed harder and drew blood from the base of Hamid's throat.

"Tokunbo!"

"Father!"

Eddie could see Barlo's face writhing, possessed by the enormous conflict of his vying emotions. The captain would make to thrust his sword all the way through to the sand, then would stop himself, then act upon the instinct once more, only to detain himself again. This back-and-forth went on for a few moments, through Oshuna's and Yewande's repeated calls, until Barlo's facial turmoil reconciled into a stony gaze.

"Bring the chains, Clayton!" he yelled. "Know this, villain: There is a part of me what wants to kill you outright! But I am letting win today the part of me that will not debase myself to your level. Instead, you will be bound as once I was when there were those who would make of me a slave.

Ropes, it seems, are not enough. Bound you shall be in chains, as bound you are to your treachery."

Antonio helped James Clayton with the chains, treating Hamid as roughly as they could while they bound him and led him back to the brig. Hamid shouted something in Arabic, which Jabari translated.

"He say you are a coward for not killing him."

Barlo laughed. "I'll show him a lot more of my cowardice later."

Oshuna had approached the captain. "You made the right decision. But I will also say that at this point I care not one whit what happens to him."

"Thank you for showing mercy, father," said Yewande. "I am proud that you could do so in such circumstances."

"The thanks go all around," responded the captain, "and especially to Mr. Eddie Fife, who, as Mr. Ola put it, 'is good with a knife.'"

"Woe to the uninvited who dare intrude on our wedding," said Bronwen, "for Mr. Fife defends his spouses fiercely."

She embraced Eddie, and Yewande, too.

"Does it make us both Mrs. Fife?" Bronwen asked with a wink.

Yewande laughed and then said, suddenly serious, "I think we should choose a new surname. Isn't that what you did, father?"

"Indeed. I wanted a new name for my new life. Perhaps that is fitting for the three of you as well."

Captain Barlo looked at the sun approaching the western horizon and let out a deep breath. "Now, take my blessing, all of you, for my men and I, the skinners, must depart. Eddie, take good care of your new family. May it grow. Higgins, take good care of the Sea Witch and her brave community. Oshuna, Yewande, Bronwen, please know that in my estimation, you need no taking care of—I only ask your understanding and tolerance when we men say such things to each other, for we know what we are about."

Oshuna was the first to laugh at this, and then Karaya, and Marie, and finally all the women together.

"We tolerate you men, sure enough," said Yewande, "the way you men must also tolerate us women: 'tis a mix of frustration with appreciation."

"Before I was so rudely distracted from our ceremony of union," said Eddie, taking the hands of his new spouses, "I was in a state of sincere and simple marvel for these two beautiful, wonderful women, and even beyond that, of marvel for our ceremony, for this community, and for our lives here. Go in peace, Captain Barlo, and return soon. Share with us as we make of all this a New World."

Shortly thereafter, the three newly- and nudelyweds stood on the edge of the surf with their arms around each other, watching the *Capricorn* sail away into the setting sun.

Afterword

While naturism or social nudism is an early-twentieth-century movement associated with Europe, all human societies have had contexts for social nudism. As a specialist in Latin America, I've been fascinated by the ingenuity and resilience of cimarron communities. They were settlements of people who had fled slavery, living off the land as far as possible from the colonial authorities. Such communities are known as *quilombos* in Brazil, *palenques* in Cuba and Colombia, *comarcas* in Ecuador, and several other names as well. These communities are not known to have functioned without clothing, yet it is easy to imagine that their needs related to clothing could have been quite different from European norms.

Determined to honor the heritage of those who fought to free themselves from enslavement, and to contribute more to understanding the vital history of Africans in the Americas, I began thinking about the motives that people living in such communities might have had for not wearing clothes. I came to imagine the Caribbean as the intersection of many outcasts united in their essential search for liberty—the same people that the colonial powers had trouble pinning down: pirates and buccaneers, cimarrons and former enslaved people, immigrants and diasporas of many kinds. The Caribbean, vast and open and faraway from Europe, became a center for rebellion against European mores, not only of church and state, but also of social customs, including dress. After all, the basin of the Caribbean (unlike the Mediterranean) lies entirely within the tropics; it's certainly warm enough to live the clothes-free life, as attested by the many nudist and nude-friendly resorts and cruises in the Caribbean today.

To more deeply familiarize myself with the history and culture of the Caribbean and the role of cimarron communities, I gleaned valuable insights from Carrie Gibson's *Empire's Crossroads*, Eduardo Galeano's *Espejos*, Frank Moya Pons' *History of the Caribbean*, and Antonio Benítez-Rojo's *La isla que se repite*. On the more specific topic of pirates and buccaneers, I found terrific information in Colin Woodard's *The Republic of Pirates*. To capture something of the pirate ambiance and lingo as expressed in literature, I read and reread widely, from Robert Louis Stevenson's classic *Treasure Island* to M. S. Hunter's historical-erotic *The Buccaneer*, to the more recent *Love and Other Pranks* by Tony Vigorito (a terrific novel). Most influential of all has been Tim Powers' spectacular *On Stranger Tides*, acknowledged not only as the source for the fourth *Pirates of the Caribbean* film specifically, but also as the model for the plots and atmosphere of the film franchise in general.

Several sources document certain pirates' penchant for using appearance to intimidate, preferring to avoid the expenditure of precious lives and ammunition if possible. The sources also show that same-sex unions were not uncommon among pirates, and as to the matter of polyamorous relationships, we know they have always existed, sanctioned in some societies and outside the law in others. A literary precursor in the Greater Caribbean for a kind of polyamorous triad relationship can be found in Teresa de la Parra's novel *Memorias de Mamá Blanca*.

New World fauna, flora, foods and technologies are highlighted in *Skinners*, such as the coati, the macaw, iguanas, the aloe plant, popcorn, the tumpline and the *bohíos*—the thatched dwellings of the indigenous peoples of the Caribbean. Christopher Columbus mistook manatees for mermaids, as recorded in his log, the *Diario de a bordo*. Much of my information about zemis, or *cemíes*, the sacred objects kept by the Taino and other Indigenous peoples of the Caribbean, comes from Serge Gruzinski's *Images at War*. These Indigenous Caribbeans did indeed send the

Spaniards island-hopping for gold as a way of getting rid of them. The Spaniards went on to set up the first global empire, and when they arrived in the Visayan islands in the nation now known as the Philippines, they were amazed by the tattoos of the people who lived there and called them *pintados*.

Cultural elements that Africans brought to the New World play an important role in *Skinners*, and several specific incidents in the plot are inspired by historical documentation. These range from obvious contributions in food (okra, millet, and other crops) and music (the drumming cadences and capoeira-like martial arts) to more subtle aspects of lived experience. The practice of fugitives keeping seeds in their hair, for example, is described in Galeano's *Espejos*. Owo and Osogbo are centuries-old cities in the majority Yoruba-speaking area of what is now southwestern Nigeria. Osogbo, where Oshuna is from, is the historical center of worship of Oshun, the *orisha* (divinity) of beauty, love, femininity, fertility, and divination. The character Oshuna is very deliberately evocative of these traits. The blending of African religious beliefs and practices with Catholicism (as well as certain Indigenous elements) is known as syncretism, a formative aspect in the development of societies in the Caribbean and Brazil, particularly. Also well documented is the existence of African pirates who escaped slavery in the Caribbean and gained positions of power in multi-ethic crews. The best known of these was Black Caesar, active in the early 1700s. I feel it is necessary to state that the rape, abuse, torture, and murder of enslaved people has also been widely documented.

Words and phrases I've used in Yoruba (as well as those in French, Italian and other languages) are accurate as far as my understanding allows. Singing or humming as a way of relating the body to a location—a song map—is an idea I explored in *Aglow* and wanted to express again here, although for a different objective.

I've embraced the term "historical-speculative" as the most appropriate for categorizing this novel, as well as for my previous novel *Aglow*. Both are more historical than speculative, but all of *Skinners*, and the historical part of *Aglow*, are speculative in the sense that they present imagined contexts for, and outcomes of, social nudism in different historical settings. While there is also a recognized literary category called "alternate history," my work in *Skinners* and *Aglow* has not explored alternate timelines so much as an alternate lifestyle—naturism or social nudism—within real historical timelines. In my application of "historical-speculative," the "speculative" part doesn't mean there are elves, or time travel, or aliens from outer space, but rather that the decisions that certain people might have made regarding social nudity, and the consequences of those decisions, may have been far more interesting than most history books would lead us to suspect.

This is one of the major contributions of fiction: pushing out the boundaries of what we can imagine to exist, or to have existed, or to be possible to exist. Frankly, we naturists who rebel against textile society do this daily in real life—nothing fictional about it! Yet naturist fiction opens other examples that are speculative, alternative, or hypothetical, perhaps, but nonetheless illustrative of our choices and their possible ramifications in the wider world.

This book would not exist as it does without feedback from partial read-throughs and comments by Allen Knudsen, Paul Walker, Lanette Clark, and Devin Knox, and from comments from readers on various posts at naturistfiction.org, a site kindly shared with me by Paul Walker and Robert Longpré. I am grateful to them all. Deep thanks also to my friend Bernard Perroud for his art that graces the cover of this book as well as the covers of my two previous novels. Many thanks to my family for their continued love and support in so many ways, and for their extraordinary patience, and many thanks to well-wishers including J L Krohnert, Ola Aralepo, Joe Jackson, Diana and Ray McCalment, Darren Shields, fellow naturist writer D H Jonathan, and many more in the terrific support network at Oaklake Trails Naturist Park. To all my readers, my sincere gratitude for forming part of the community!